MAN, FUCK THIS HOUSE

BRIAN ASMAN

A MUTATED MEDIA PRODUCTION

Man, Fuck This House
Copyright © 2021 Brian Asman

All Rights Reserved

ISBN: 978-1-7364677-2-5

Edited by Max Booth III

Cover Art by Matthew Revert

Interior Layout by Lori Michelle
www.TheAuthorsAlley.com

Also by Brian Asman

I'm Not Even Supposed to be Here Today
(Eraserhead Press)
Jailbroke
Nunchuck City

Coming Soon

Return of the Living Elves
Comic Cons

For Tobe Hooper, Shirley Jackson, and anybody who's ever seen a ghost

BEFORE

THROUGH THE UPSTAIRS windows, the House watched.

And waited.

And despaired, until every last glimmer of hope leached from its bones, the all-consuming emptiness a blight more entropic than any dry rot. Bowing its eaves, bending its beams, cracking its foundations, leaving it a cicada-skin, a vacant replica of the thing it once was, doomed to wither and flake and— battered by the dumb vagaries of man and nature alike—eventually dissolve into the wind.

And then.

Then—

SUNDAY

SHORTLY AFTER LUNCHTIME, a beige Toyota Camry took a long, lugubrious left into James Circle, the back-end sagging from the combined weight of the Haskins family and what worldly possessions weren't left for the movers.

"This is it, team!" Hal Haskins said brightly. Hal was a man whose personality favored his car's paint job, prone to dad jokes and bland observations. His hobbies included checkers, Roth IRAs, and assorted flavors of sportsball—his word. Even played a little sportsball, too, when his trick knee allowed it.

"Aren't you excited, kids?" Sabrina Haskins asked, twisting around in her seat to regard her literal two-and-a-half children—ten-year-old Damien had eaten his own twin in the womb. Or *absorbed* him, as the OB/GYN corrected, but she couldn't quite part with the notion she'd given birth to a cannibal. For years she woke up in the middle of the night, soaked in sweat, terrified she was pregnant all over again, her son digging his way out of her uterus with a pickaxe jury-rigged from his dead brother's bones, gasping for breath as her own blood rushing from the wounds, threatening to drown him—

His older sister, Michaela, barely looked up from her phone long enough to roll her eyes. "Whatever."

"Hmmph."

Sabrina was excited, even if the kids couldn't be bothered. She'd always thought of Columbus as a stop on the way to bigger and better things, but after dropping out of Ohio State mid-sophomore year to pursue her real passion—getting groped by hot sauce-fingered rednecks at Hooters—she'd gotten stuck there. Then she'd met Hal, who came in one night with his coworkers for a plate of mild wings and exactly two beers. Maybe they hadn't fallen in love, per se, but he was a good guy with a steady job selling reverse mortgages to widows. Part of her always figured something would change—what specifically she couldn't say—and then life would be somehow different. More exciting. More interesting.

But it hadn't.

Four years in Columbus turned into fourteen. Two kids, stretch marks, a series of part-time jobs and aborted stints at community college. Sabrina literally tried to get into basket weaving. BASKET WEAVING! Her other recurring nightmare involved becoming the world's foremost weaver of baskets, basically the Martha Stewart of basketry. Flying off to Paris or Dubai at a moment's notice to weave a basket for some foreign dignitary or oil sheik.

Becoming famous was one thing, but becoming famous for something so gosh-darned boring seemed like its own special kind of H-E-Double-Hockey-Sticks.

So when Hal came home from work one day and told her he'd been offered a big promotion, but they'd have to move, she didn't even ask where. Columbus was a fine town, but she needed a change so badly anywhere would be an improvement. She'd never heard of Jackson Hill, but it was apparently one of America's most desirable small cities. Whataburger had even opened a franchise there the year before! Maybe it wasn't San Fran or Seattle or even the less-murdery parts of St. Louis, but she kind of liked that. The whole city seemed like a blank envelope. Anything could be inside. She could reinvent herself, become whatever she wanted.

If only she could figure out what that was.

The Camry came to a halt outside a two-story Craftsman with brand-new siding and a slightly-overgrown yard. Across the street, in front of a house painted a very off-putting mustard-yellow, a grey-braided lady glanced up from her flowerbeds long enough to wave at the Haskins family with a pair of shears. Sabrina tried to wave back, but the lady had already looked away.

"One, two, three, break!" Hal said, shutting off the car.

Sabrina grabbed her purse off the floor and got out, legs stiff from spending the last six hours in the car, and another twelve the day before that, the trip only broken up by brief stops at gas stations and a night at a Motel 3 (*Half the price, twice the fun!*) where she'd had to leave the Gideon Bible with a confused front desk clerk because Damien wouldn't stop ripping out the pages. The fall breeze ruffled her hair pleasantly.

"Just got a text," Hal said, coming around the car. "The movers are late. Go figure, right?"

Sabrina looked at her husband and winced—powdered sugar from their gas station donut breakfast dappled his face. She slipped a crumpled napkin from her purse and dabbed his left cheek.

"I'm fine, I'm fine," Hal craned his neck away. "Geez."

"Just trying to help." Sabrina rapped on the car window. "Kids?"

Michaela reached for the handle, frowned, slapped the window.

"Sorry," Hal said, leaning back in the driver's side. "Forgot the child locks." Ever since Damien tried to bail out on the freeway, both Haskins children had had to suffer the indignity of child locks. Now freed, both took their sweet time getting out of the car. Michaela, to her credit, slipped her phone into her jeans and acted like she was part of the moment. Damien, however, stood sullenly in the driveway, staring down at his feet.

Hal dropped into a crouch next to his son. "What's wrong, champ?"

"I don't like it." The words came out cold, monotone, like most everything Damien said.

"What's not to like, buddy?"

Damien shook his head and said no more.

"Such a freak," Michaela muttered.

"I heard that, young lady," Sabrina said, then cringed because she sounded like her mother, a severe and uncompromising woman who choked to death on a California roll when Sabrina was in high school. Whenever Sabrina said anything too overtly motherly, she imagined her throat closing up, her skin turning blue, and her two children laughing their butts off while she clawed impotently at the air.

Hal hefted Damien up on his shoulders. "Come

on, let's check out our new digs. I think you'll really like it once you get your bearings." Stooped under the weight of his son, Hal staggered up the flagstones to the front door, Michaela trailing behind.

Sabrina watched her family for a moment, heart swelling—they weren't perfect, but they were HERS— then hurried to join them.

The house was unbelievable.

They—with the exception of Michaela, who rushed upstairs to inspect her unfurnished new room, and Damien, there in body but not in spirit—started with a tour of the house. The front door led to a foyer, a stairwell heading straight up to the second story. To their left was the living room, a roomy space with hardwood floors. They poked their heads in, noting the curving archway, then headed towards the kitchen—recently updated with granite countertops, a fetching grey/black backsplash, and shiny steel appliances. Even better, the counters seemed to go on for days. Another door led to the empty dining room, which connected through to the living room.

Sabrina couldn't wait to cook a meal without banging a shin or elbow on something.

"The porch," Hal declared, stepping through a door at the rear of the house—thanks to the school schedule and the speed of the move, he was the only one who'd seen the new house so far. Sabrina followed him to a screened-in porch looking out on the backyard—enclosed by a wood fence, nothing but trees beyond.

"Other side's a state park," Hal said, setting Damien down on the back steps. The boy wandered into the yard and sat in the grass, cross-legged. He commenced massacring dandelions, blowing fluff away with a soft *pooft* of his lips.

Sabrina didn't want to think about whatever the boy might be wishing for.

The yard wasn't huge, but that would make it easier to maintain. Damien could probably mow the lawn in a few passes—one of the few household chores he'd do, heavily supervised by Hal. And they had a shiny metal shed, one of those pre-fab jobs. Maybe she could take up gardening. Get their new neighbor, the old lady with the shears, to give her some pointers, finally turn that black thumb green.

"Can we see the upstairs?" Sabrina asked.

Hal nodded. "Wait'll you see the master bedroom." He cupped a hand to the side of his mouth. "Let's go, buddy!"

Damien didn't even look up.

"He's fine," Sabrina said, grabbing Hal by the arm. Together they went back in through the kitchen.

Passing the stairs, Sabrina noted a door she hadn't seen on the way in. "Where's that go?"

"Basement?" Hal said, but it sounded more like a question than a statement.

Sabrina shrugged it off, she wanted to get a look at the bedrooms first. Specifically hers. If they'd re-done the master bath like the kitchen—

Hal stomped up the stairs. "They sure don't make them like this anymore. Solid, solid construction. This thing'll still be standing when we're long gone, I'll tell you that."

MAN, FUCK THIS HOUSE

Sabrina froze in her tracks, gooseflesh standing up on her arms. The idea of the house outlasting not only her and Hal, but her children too, seemed perverse. But that wasn't all. *Long gone* was totally relative. The house need not survive into some far-flung future, when polar bears were extinct and the Eastern seaboard lay completely underwater, fish swimming in-and-out of the broken windows of submerged IKEAs. If the Haskins family dropped off the face of the earth that very day, the house'd only have to stand a few years longer to make Hal's Confauxian wisdom come true.

What's long gone, *anyway?*

"'Brina?" Hal called from the top of the stairs.

What the hell had gotten into her? She hadn't had thoughts like these in a long time, not since the months directly after Damien's birth.

"Coming," she replied, taking the stairs two at a time. He was waiting at the landing. A door to the right leaned open, revealing the children's bathroom. She poked her head in and cringed—the tub, sink and tile all looked older, maybe not original but definitely not updated like the kitchen, plus the old owners had left them a shower curtain, a clear plastic, duck-emblazoned affair Michaela was sure to LOVE.

Maybe she wouldn't be using this bathroom, but she couldn't help but feel disappointed, it certainly wasn't as lovely as the rest of the house.

Hal pushed open the next door. "I was thinking this could be Damien's room."

"Sure." She found she didn't really care to see the rest of the house—too worried the master bath would be a late '80s travesty like the kids' bathroom.

The door across from Damien's was wide open, a slightly-bigger facsimile with purple curtains hanging over the windows. "This was supposed to be Michaela's," Hal mumbled, his head slowly swiveling to the door at the end of the hall.

The CLOSED door at the end of the hall.

"Don't get too comfortable in there," Sabrina called, although her daughter probably had her AirPods shoved firmly in either ear. She advanced quickly down the hall and flung the door open.

The room was empty, the only movement from the lazily-circling ceiling fan.

Sabrina crossed the room, poked her head into the master bath. She barely had time to feel relief at the glossy teal tile, the Whirlpool tub, the separate shower stall—features she'd coveted for YEARS—because Michaela wasn't there either.

"That your dream bathroom or what, hun?" Hal said. "Imagine soaking in that tub, some candles, red wine, *me*—"

Sabrina turned. "Where's Michaela?"

Hal shrugged. "Around?"

"Michaela?" Sabrina called, her voice echoing off the walls.

Down the hallway, a toilet flushed. A beat later, a door creaked open.

"Mom!" Michaela yelled. "There's no soap, give me the hand sanitizer."

Sabrina frowned, digging in her purse until she found the small plastic bottle of GermX, and headed back down the hall. Michaela stuck both hands out in a gesture that seemed plaintive, despite her demanding tone.

MAN, FUCK THIS HOUSE

"Give me the hand sanitizer, *please*," Sabrina said, pushing the bottle into her daughter's hands.

"Whatever." Michaela squirted gel into one palm and handed the bottle back, then walked off down the hall rubbing her hands together. "Which one's mine?"

"Right here, monkey," Hal said.

"Ugh, don't call me that." Michaela's door slammed.

Sabrina turned to Hal. "That was weird."

"Par for the course, she's practically a teenager."

"No, that's not what I mean." Sabrina cocked her chin at the master bedroom. "I thought she was in our room."

"Why would she be in our room?"

"I don't know." Something about the last few minutes didn't track. Maybe Michaela had come downstairs while they'd been in the backyard, gone out to the car or something.

Must have, Sabrina thought. She stepped into the kids' bathroom, thinking she'd leave her sanitizer on the sink until they unpacked and found the hand soap. A little surprised Michaela didn't have a cutting remark ready about the childish, duck-covered shower curtain—

The second Sabrina stepped into the bathroom, it all made sense. And didn't.

A plain white shower curtain hung where the ducks had been.

The second Damien was absolutely sure nobody was watching, he stopped picking stupid dandelions and slipped behind the shed, pulling his phone from his pants pocket.

Fortnite time!

Damien lived for these moments, when no one was watching. He'd never felt particularly comfortable in his own skin, until he was six and heard a lady on TV talking about something called an *old soul.* That fit him to a tee. He wasn't completely uninterested in childish things—he lived for a silly multiplayer shooter filled with goofy fish people and exploding llamas—but he'd always been wiser, smarter, and more mature than his years. A committed rationalist, he didn't believe in past lives *per se,* but he often got flashes of fabricated memories that led him to believe he played a role in the Renaissance. Not Leonardo, or Michelangelo, or anyone famous enough to become a Ninja Turtle five centuries later, but some tangential bit player who maybe painted a fresco in a shed on the Vatican grounds or something.

Because he was so perceptive, from a young age he picked up on how Sabrina looked at him—like a freak. He'd overheard her and his father arguing once, and while he didn't understand everything they were talking about, he looked up *parasitic twin* online and was taken aback. Somehow, Sabrina thought it was HIS fault, that HE bore responsibility for the viability of the other fetus with whom he'd briefly shared a womb. As if a naturally-occurring phenomenon was somehow strange, or evil, or just plain intentional. His own brain had barely formed at the time. Reabsorption simply *happened.*

And yet she called him a cannibal.

MAN, FUCK THIS HOUSE

Never mind that he hadn't actually EATEN the other twin—one would think a half-college educated woman might have some inkling of what went on inside her own body, but no. Damien wasn't a particularly fearful child, but one thing that scared the absolute bejeezus out of him was the ignorance of adults. Forget Santa Claus, that plump and preposterous pseudo-deity he'd never even for a second believed in (okay, *one time,* but he was three, and he really, REALLY wanted that Big Hug Elmo. For science, totally for science), the biggest lie he'd believed as a child was that adults knew what they were doing.

They absolutely did not.

In Damien's eyes, the dividing line betwixt adult and child was simply how self-serious one was. Children thought the moon was made of cheese; adults believed in more complex but equally silly things, like government. Everything was one big joke.

So Damien decided to play the biggest one he could think of.

Convincing Sabrina he was a precocious but decidedly non-evil child was a waste of time—she'd named him after the hellspawn in *The Omen,* after all. No, he'd lean into it. Act strange, aloof. Creepy, even.

His own private joke on the world, and the fools who'd brought him into it.

They had no idea he liked *Fortnite,* peanut butter and banana sandwiches, and the flipping *Wiggles,* of all things (a musical group he appreciated ironically, of course). Only his sister Michaela, his sole confidant, knew the real Damien.

Hence his behavior on the front lawn. He'd hoped

to unsettle his parents with a single, unexplained comment—*I don't like it*—and he'd easily succeeded. After, Sabrina seemed distracted, fearful.

Time to celebrate.

He tried to open the *Fortnite* app, but only had one bar. A quick search of the neighbor's WiFi networks yielded nothing, unsecured or otherwise. The Haskins family network wouldn't be set up until at least mid-week, if not later. He was about to wander inside to lick the baseboards or stand silently in the corner of the living room when his phone beeped. He figured it was a friend from back home—Marshall or Faroukh, both two grades above him and bright for their age, about as mature friends as a ten-year-old could hope to make. But he didn't recognize the number, and the area code was local to Jackson Hill.

Odd.

Damien opened the message. It simply said, *Sup?*

He wondered if a neighboring kid had somehow gotten his number—maybe from his parents, most likely his idiot father because Sabrina at least had the good sense not to inflict her demonic child upon others. Hal was always trying to make friends for him, sometimes with hilarious results, like the time he'd bought a bunch of ice cream from Baskin Robbins and tried to talk some kids at the playground into coming to Damien's seventh birthday party (Damien, for his part, had blown out the candles on his cake never knowing one of his greatest wishes had come true— at that moment, his father was sitting broken-nosed and black-eyed in a jail cell, charged with attempted kidnapping, while the parents who beat the living snot out of him got off scot-free).

MAN, FUCK THIS HOUSE

Damien considered the single-word message for a long moment, then decided anyone who'd text a new acquaintance something as banal and flat-out lazy as *sup* didn't merit a response. He slipped out from behind the shed, straightening his posture into the rigid, straight-legged robotic walk he used whenever Sabrina might be watching.

His phone buzzed again.

I asked you a question, little man. Straight up rude.

Damien had quite a few opinions on that—rude in *his* book was texting a stranger out of the blue and acting as if one were entitled to his time—but decided not to enlighten the mysterious texter on the finer points of *etiquette a la Haskins*.

Once again, a text popped up.

I can see you ignoring me.

Damien's heart thumped. Clutching his phone tightly to his chest, he turned around in a slow circle, expecting some teenaged goofus to be hanging over the fence, but he didn't see anyone, and he didn't think anyone at the windows of the neighboring houses could see directly into the backyard where he stood.

For once, the unsettling boy was himself unsettled, and Damien didn't care for that one bit.

Who is this? What do you want?

A set of ellipses popped up, indicating his—*stalker* seemed hysterical, but discomfortingly accurate—mystery texter was writing what looked like a long response. Damien stood there in the middle of the yard, waiting for the response to come through.

But it didn't.

He shot a nervous glance up at the house, hoping Sabrina wouldn't see him doing something so quotidian as having a text message conversation. Luckily the rest of the family seemed preoccupied. He turned his attention back to the phone, those cursed ellipses—threatening another strange and overly-familiar message.

After five minutes, he headed inside. As he grabbed the screen door, his phone pinged once again.

The message was short, but easily the most unnerving yet.

You'll see.

The movers arrived, eventually—just as the sun dipped down behind the mustard-yellow house across the street—lugging the Haskins' possessions into the house with a supreme disregard for the brand-new paint job, scraping incoherent graffiti into the walls with bedframes and wardrobes. Sabrina tried to redirect the men, but they paid little attention, and she quickly resigned herself to stopping by Home Depot with a few paint chips to try to match the house's hues.

Despite the collateral damage, the movers were efficient, unloading their stuff in an hour. Hal dithered over tipping the men or simply offering them a beer, but they waved him off, leaving the Haskins family alone. Sabrina tried not to feel *too* overwhelmed by the massive amount of things they needed to do. She decided to get the kitchen situated first, ripping open the heavy cardboard boxes and finding homes for forks, pans, and spatulae, marveling at kitchen gadgets she couldn't remember packing and hadn't used in years.

A loud bang echoed through the open window, followed by a yelp and some very inventive cursing. Sabrina looked out into the backyard—her husband pogoed around on one leg, clutching his shin, the shed doors open and the family mower waiting patiently just below the raised, six-inch lip. Hal hopped around in a circle, then rubbed his shin, face red. Then— gingerly, limping—Hal grabbed the mower's handle, pushed down so the wheels cleared that little step up into the shed, and muscled the mower into its new home.

Sabrina smiled, shaking her head. Hal could be a real goof sometimes.

But he was HER goof.

The rest of the day passed in a flurry of activity— its nadir the moment Hal presented her with ANOTHER box marked KITCHEN STUFF, requiring a near-total reconfiguration of the work she'd already done—and by nightfall, even though they still had a lot to do, the house felt at least a little bit like home. Sabrina took Hal's car to the store, bought groceries, and cooked their first meal—a pretty okay pot roast with baked potatoes and veggies. After dinner, Sabrina even coaxed the kids—plus her husband, who'd found the local AM sports station and had become otherwise useless—into playing a family game of Monopoly. Even Damien, who usually shunned family time but could be talked into it if there was money involved, fake or otherwise.

Even when Sabrina landed her thimble on Park Place, dotted with Damien's hotels, and had to pay him an exorbitant sum to kick free, she didn't mind. For once, the whole family sat together, talking and laughing and pretending they liked each other.

This, Sabrina thought, *this is what real families are like.*

Later, falling asleep, she wondered if maybe, just maybe, a change was all they needed, and from now on, in this strange new town called Jackson Hill, everything would be fine.

Right before everything went black, she could've sworn she heard a voice whisper NO.

The Haskins family slept.

The house did not.

MONDAY

THIRTY MINUTES BEFORE noon, it finally occurred to Sabrina that she could actually sit down.

The morning passed by in a whirlwind. Up by six, packing lunches and making sure every member of the family had what they needed to get where they were going, and dodging all of the boxed possessions they'd yet to put away. Effectively fighting both her children, a two-fronted verbal fencing match where both Michaela and an oddly-verbose Damien trotted out a laundry list of reasons why they shouldn't have to start school yet, not on their THIRD day in Jackson Hill. Inhumane, according to the younger Haskinses—prisoners of war could expect better treatment.

Meanwhile, Hal couldn't find his shaving kit, then his pants. Finally walked downstairs wearing a shirt/sport coat combo that made Sabrina cringe, but she gave him a peck on the cheek and sent him on his way, a brown bag lunch tucked in the briefcase he only carried because his elderly clients expected it from him.

Getting the kids on their way was a much more difficult proposition, and Sabrina briefly considered handcuffing them together so neither would get lost, but given they were headed to separate schools that would've presented all manner of difficulties. Finally, she got them out the door, reminding them she could easily see the bus stop from the living room window.

"Fine, just don't come out here," Michaela said, rolling her eyes. She grabbed her little brother's hand and dragged him out the door.

Good as her word, Sabrina peeled back the drapes and watched them amble to the bus stop at the end of the street. No other children waited next to the stop sign. Sabrina wondered if the other neighbors even *had* kids—somebody must, in a cul-de-sac with four houses—and if the other parents drove their kids to school. That got her wondering if there was some sort of carpool she could join. Her own Sienna hadn't arrived yet, shipped cross-country separately since LifeCrate didn't handle automobiles. Granted she had enough to do around the house and no urgent errands to run, but the delayed delivery of her car stretched out the move, when she only wanted to get settled into their new life.

The elementary bus pulled up. Damien managed to board without biting anyone. Michaela sat with her back against the stop sign and played with her phone until the next bus came.

After spying on her kids, Sabrina made more coffee and set about organizing the never-ending boxes of Haskins *stuff*. Much of the morning was spent reorganizing her own closet—the walk-in she'd always wanted—and transferring Hal's old sporting equipment to new boxes bound for Goodwill. What did a right-handed man need THREE left-handed gloves for? She did the same with some old toys the kids insisted on saving—they wouldn't notice. Kind of irritated her. Couldn't they have gotten rid of half this junk back in Columbus? But she'd learned to pick her battles over the years.

Since her Sienna hadn't arrived, Sabrina had hidden the giveaway boxes somewhere they wouldn't be discovered. The basement, which she hadn't even taken a look at yet, seemed perfect. Sweating profusely, she carried one of the heavier junk boxes into the hallway and set it down. She opened the basement door, a gaping black void in front of her. She groped for the light, reaching into darkness. Shivered, imagining her hand brushing up against another, cold fingers entwining her own—

Her hand found the drawstring.

A single bulb illuminated the stairwell, a cramped space with rickety stairs and rusting nails stuck in the walls. Sabrina put a foot down and tested the stairs—sturdier than they looked—and figured she'd go down to the basement first, confirm there was somewhere to put—

Wham, wham, wham!

Sabrina jumped at the knocks. She turned off the light and shut the basement door. Who could be knocking? Other than the gardening lady on Saturday, she'd not seen any of the neighbors, and no welcome wagon had stopped by the previous evening—but maybe the other folks who lived in James Circe were overly respectful rather than weird or reclusive, of course a family wouldn't want company on their first full day in a new house.

Sabrina put her eye to the peephole, couldn't see

anything but a vague smear of shadow. "Hello?" she called.

"It's your neighbor," a friendly yet strong female voice replied.

Sabrina opened the door to find the older gardener standing on the stoop with a cellophane-wrapped plate of sandwiches.

"In Finland they call these porilainen. My own recipe, kale, seitan, onions and cucumber with avocado yogurt. Zephyr Rubens, by the way," she said, offering a heavily-bejeweled hand.

Sabrina gave it a quick shake, apprising her new neighbor. The woman had icy blue eyes and looked like she'd been reverse-mugged by the QVC Network. Topaz dangled from her ears, six or seven equally-bejeweled necklaces hung around her leathery neck. Bangles bangled at her wrists. Sabrina couldn't see the woman's feet beneath her flowy, multi-colored skirt, but she probably sported as many toe-rings as toes on which to put them.

"Sabrina," Sabrina said. "Haskins. Nice to meet you, um, Zephyr. That's an interesting name."

"David Crosby gave it to me in 1972. Before then—oh, but I here I am telling you my life story, and on the front porch. May I come in?" Zephyr wiggled the tray of porilainen.

Sabrina blushed. "What was I thinking? Of course you can." She stepped aside, motioning her neighbor into the living room.

Zephyr took a single step then paused, toe over the threshold, a stricken look gripping her face. "I—" She stepped back, holding out her sandwich tray. "Terribly sorry, I just remembered a previous engagement. We'll have to catch up another time. My place, maybe? I make the most delicious kava tea, you *must* try it."

"Okay." Sabrina took the plate and stood there awkwardly. "Maybe I'll come by tomorrow."

Zephyr nodded quickly. "Do that. Bye now." She turned and hurried off down the front steps, taking them two at a time.

Sabrina watched her cross the cul-de-sac, never once looking back.

What an odd duck.

But at least she brought sandwiches.

The porcelain—whatever they were called—were terrible.

Sabrina could barely stomach the one, and only finished it because her upbringing disallowed her from wasting even a morsel of perfectly-good food. The kale and Satan or whatever it was called tasted like dirt, ACTUAL DIRT, and she'd found herself hovering over the kitchen trash, ready to toss it in after one bite. Ultimately she choked the rest of the sandwich down, then performed some serious surgery on its fellows, picking off the kale, frying up real bacon, smashing the bread together and turning them into BLTs, more or less. She felt terrible, doing all that to such a thoughtful gift, but at the same time no one else would be eating them if she didn't do *something.*

Was everyone in Jackson Hill like Zephyr, aging hippies who ate awful food and talked about their auras? What could she possibly have in common with them?

What do you have in common with anyone? said the sneaky little voice in the back of her head.

Sabrina stretched the cellophane back over her improvised BLTs and put them in the fridge, along with a post-it that said EAT ME next to a tiny drawing of a dinosaur. A T-Rex, just an outline but still recognizable, jaws yawning open. She'd always liked doodling, as long as she could remember. How she met Hal, in fact. That first night at Hooter's, when she'd been an orange-shorted waitress and he a young reverse mortgage salesman at Mor-Gone, she caricatured the man seated next to him, a smallish, thin man with the sort of hook nose that SCREAMED for cartoonification—Hal's boss, it turned out. On some strange impulse she still couldn't understand herself—she would've surely been fired if humorless Mr. Teague had seen the drawing and complained to her manager—she slipped her sketch to Hal. Later, with his crew of office drones dispersing, he cornered her near the wait station and the rest was history.

Haskins family history.

Sabrina sometimes wondered what life would be like if she hadn't drawn that picture. If she'd drawn other, better pictures. Followed her true passion of taking over the *Peanuts* comic strip from Charles Schulz—a silly dream, maybe, but now, with the Internet, who knows what might've happened?

Nothing, the voice said.

She slammed the refrigerator shut and returned to her interrupted task—the basement. Unfinished, utilitarian, cement floors and exposed wiring, maybe half the size of the first floor. The washer/dryer sat at the bottom of the steps, the furnace opposite. A dark alcove—probably a crawlspace—lay beyond. Faint light shown through the two windows, dust motes dancing in the weak rays. Mildew hung in the air.

No family room in waiting, this, but the boxes of excess Haskins stuff could be easily stowed, and once her car arrived, she could get rid of it all. Really Mary Kanto it, like that guru her old friends were so enamored of.

Sabrina turned for the stairs, and froze.

A man was coming down the steps. A BIG man, well over six feet, with equally broad shoulders and a bulging belly hanging out over his ratty sweatpants. His cheeks flushed red, and he had the kind of doughy, simple face incapable of expressing guile or malice.

Part of her wanted to scream, but he looked kind and carried the box of Hal's old sports junk.

"Where do you want this?"

Lips moving soundlessly, Sabrina simply pointed to the wall where the other boxes were stacked.

The man nodded, carried the box over and set it down in the indicated spot. He grunted, straightening himself, then ran a hand over one of the older boxes, staring placidly up at the window.

Then he walked, trudged really, over to the furnace and hefted his big body up and over the cement wall into the crawlspace.

Sabrina gaped. Nothing about what happened made sense. If he were a mover, maybe one of the LifeCrate men returned out of a sense of altruism to help the Haskins family get settled, why would he enter without knocking, and even more importantly WHY IN THE WORLD DID HE CRAWL INTO THE CRAWLSPACE?

She ran across the basement, house slippers slapping on the concrete, and peered into the crawlspace—small, dank, lousy with torn-up insulation.

Hardly big enough for her.

Let alone the man who was no longer there.

School, as per usual, proved a welcome respite from the stress of family life. At home, Damien had to constantly be *on,* lest he inadvertently reveal his true nature to Sabrina. At school he could relax, a little, even though he had to remind himself not to blurt out the answers or condescend to the teacher who usually knew far less than he about any given subject. The flattening of any truly interesting bit of history into a neat, pat narrative—the sociopolitical complexity of early-twentieth-century Europe, for example, in the years before Gavrilo Princip fired his fatal shot into the neck of Archduke Franz Ferdinand, received only a passing acknowledgment from his old fifth-grade teacher in Columbus. Why they continued to employ him, rather than simply play Dan Carlin's *Hardcore History* episodes on the subject, baffled Damien.

Still, his first day at Freeling Elementary seemed a qualified success. He'd befriended a few other kids, waxed poetic on his favorite *Fortnite* drops and showed them some of the rare skins in his locker like Black Knight—some of his new friends hadn't even been *allowed* to play *Fortnite* back when that skin debuted. Damien found the idea of modulating one's behavior based on parental diktat utterly hilarious, but kept his composure so as not to alienate his new friends, who were all very nice but definitely standard-issue small town children.

Too, he'd received no additional messages from the odd and overly-familiar texter, which made him think it had all been some misunderstanding.

When the bus pulled up at the stop near James Circle, he said his goodbyes to the bus driver—a dangerous move, if Sabrina ever conversed with the woman he could be exposed as a thoughtful and caring child—and composed his features into the usual slack, vaguely-menacing expression he employed around Sabrina. He trudged up the street, stopping at the end of the driveway to stare up at his new house.

All part of the game—instead of simply walking inside and proceeding to his room, he liked to wait for Sabrina to notice him watching the house like some kind of idiot burglar rather than an actual resident.

After ten minutes he gave up and walked inside.

The house was completely silent but for the floorboards creaking under his own weight. Damien frowned—they usually had a TV on somewhere, plus Sabrina banging pots and pans together, Swiffering the stairs, or crying softly in her room where she thought no one could hear her.

But now? Nothing.

He walked towards the kitchen, giving the wooden chair braced under the basement doorknob a sidelong glance—rats, perhaps? He stuck his head through the doorway. No one in the kitchen, either. Perhaps Sabrina was out ingratiating herself to the neighbors. Which Damien very much approved of, the woman needed hobbies.

Seemed he had the house all to himself, an all-too-rare event. Perhaps he'd indulge in some *SpongeBob*. Damien turned back towards the living room—

And almost screamed.

Sabrina stood in the hallway, pale and sweaty, a threadbare blanket wrapped around her. Visibly shaking. Her eyes looked sunken, dark.

Damien took an instinctive step back, not wanting to risk whatever illness she'd contracted.

"How was school?" Sabrina asked—a question she'd long ago given up asking him.

Damien forgot himself for a moment, answered with a simple, normally-inflected "Good."

Sabrina nodded, more to herself than in response to what he'd said. "Don't, um. Don't go in the basement, okay? There's—standing water."

Damien stared back at her blankly, giving a single nod to show he understood. Ordinarily he'd do more to unsettle her, but she seemed quite out of sorts already. Sabrina seemed to have frozen in the hallway. Between her and the chair barricading the basement door, there wasn't much room to maneuver, so he slipped into the dining room and back around through the living room. He hurried up the stairs, troubled by Sabrina's strange behavior. HE was supposed to be the weird one.

As he reached the landing, a voice called, "Damien?"

Sabrina stood at the bottom of the stairs, looking

up at him. A little bit of color had returned to her face, and her eyes seemed to focus on him this time, rather than merely looking past him.

"Yes?" he said, reflexively, natural emotion leeching into what should have been a monotone response.

"I'm glad you're home."

Damien smiled—against his will, actually *smiled*—and backed away up the stairs.

Something was definitely very wrong.

Sabrina lay in bed, Hal next to her with a David Baldacci novel and his Rite Aid reading glasses perched on his nose—the smudges achingly visible from her vantage point. She wanted to pluck the glasses off his face, clean them with the hem of her nightgown, but such doting drove him crazy, made him act like a Golden Retriever at bath time.

She looked down at her own reading material—last month's issue of *People*—and tried to focus on the interview with Elisabeth Moss, but the words all ran together on the page.

She couldn't focus. How could she?

The rest of the day passed in a dream-like state. A trance, maybe—she imagined hypnosis might feel like this. After debating whether to call the cops—and tell them WHAT, exactly—she'd spent several hours in the front yard, picking at the landscaping with a trowel in a pantomime of productivity. Eventually she got a sunburn on the back of her neck and was forced inside.

That's when she had the bright idea to barricade the

basement door. Maybe it wouldn't stop the large man who was somehow capable of disappearing into a tiny crawlspace, but it made her feel better. Good enough that she could grab a blanket and sit on the couch, rocking back and forth, shaking like she had the flu.

Some of that might have been the sunburn.

By the time Damien came home—and she was actually *glad* to see him, so perverse was her afternoon—the tension in her muscles was fading, she'd begun convincing herself she hadn't ACTUALLY seen a man in the basement. Ghosts didn't exist, and if they did they certainly didn't concern themselves with bored college dropouts who couldn't accept the fact they'd accidentally become homemakers. Sabrina went over everything she'd done that morning, what she'd eaten—maybe the eggs had gone south? Double-checked the carbon monoxide detectors, in case deadly fumes were messing with her mind.

Thankfully nothing.

She'd read somewhere—*Cosmo,* maybe—that sometimes the mind, without proper stimulation, will choose to stimulate itself. Make up flights of fancy, even hallucinations, out of utter boredom. But that wasn't her, how could she be bored when there was so much work to do to get the new house presentable?

After Damien trudged up to his room, Sabrina caught a glimpse of herself in the hall mirror. She looked crazy, and the blockaded basement door was a physical testament to her insanity. Grudgingly, she put the chair back in its place in the dining room before Michaela got home, went upstairs to fix her makeup.

MAN, FUCK THIS HOUSE

The rest of the evening passed in a typical domestic fashion—minor arguments over homework and vegetables and chores—and now she finally had Hal to herself. Part of her wanted to tell him everything about the Experience, and her bizarre, tension-ridden afternoon.

But another part of her wanted something else altogether.

Sabrina gave Hal's arm a light stroke. The tiny hairs stood on end, a shiver convulsed his body.

"Ooh," he said, dog-earing his current page.

Afterward, her head resting on his chest, pleasantly spent—Hal and her had always clicked, physically, and unlike some of the guys she dated in her Hooters days he definitely gave as good as he got, and then some—Sabrina's eyes fluttered shut, she was drifting off, when the bedroom door banged open.

Sabrina screamed.

The big man from the basement stood in the doorway, FILLED the doorway, holding a cardboard box. Smiling, he approached the bed, waggling his eyebrows.

Sabrina sat frozen, her mouth hanging open from the scream still resounding in her ears.

Something inside the box moved, a slight straining at the packing tape, and then with a slight *schhhrip* the tape parted, the box peeling open, *yawning* open, and whatever was in the box Sabrina didn't want to see, dear God she didn't want to see—

"Hun?"

Sabrina blinked. The man and his box were gone, she was lying in bed with her husband, the covers twisted around her legs.

Hal stared at her, brow furrowed. "Everything okay?"

Sabrina swallowed, heart racing, looked around the room. Everything seemed in its proper place, the door shut. And Hal could be oblivious at times, but no way he'd miss a sizable man barging into the bedroom.

Especially post-coitus.

"I think so," Sabrina managed.

Clearly, she'd imagined everything. And if she'd imagined that, it stood to reason she'd imagined the Experience, earlier. But why? Overactive imagination? Or something worse? Something like a brain—

No. She didn't want to think it.

"I used to get that falling dream a lot," Hal said, leaning back into the pillows. "You know, the one where you're drifting off to sleep and all of a sudden—BAM! You jerk awake, and man, back to square one?" He gazed wistfully at the ceiling, fondly remembering all the times he'd startled awake.

"I remember," Sabrina said. He'd almost knocked her out of bed while pregnant with Michaela. Thankfully, she'd caught herself on the frame of their old four-poster.

"Was it like that?"

Sabrina shook her head slightly. It would be easy, so easy, to tell Hal *yes, like that*. And he'd mix some sports metaphors and they'd turn off the bedside light and fall easily into their respective slumbers.

Except there was a box of Hal's old sporting equipment sitting down in the basement, one she'd never put there.

MAN, FUCK THIS HOUSE

Someone had.

"Hal?"

Something about her tone must have gotten his attention, because he looked at her sharply, pushed himself up onto a forearm. "What, hun?"

Sabrina worried at the hem of their comforter, trying to figure out the right way to ask what she wanted. A way that wouldn't make her sound crazy. Finally, she said, "Do you know who owned this house before us?"

"Yeah, the bank."

"Oh." Definitely explained the deal they'd gotten. "Before that?"

"Didn't ask. Probably someone upside down on their mortgage. Buy low, sell high, right?" He did a little fist-bump in the air.

Well, that didn't help. At the same time, the answer wasn't dispositive—at least he didn't tell her the previous owners were murdered, hacked to death in the very bedroom where they lay.

Or the basement.

She shivered, wrapped the comforter tightly around her body.

"Hun, are you sure you're okay?"

She wasn't going to say anything, she knew how it would sound, she really really wasn't going to say anything and then—

Then.

"Hal, do you believe in ghosts?"

Outside Hal and Sabrina's bedroom door, Damien turned to his sister, a smirk creeping into his normally-impassive features.

"Told you she's gone crazy."

TUESDAY

MICHAELA COULDN'T SLEEP.

Her bed didn't feel right, even though it was the same mattress from her old room in Columbus, she just tossed and turned and bunched up her pillow underneath her, kicked the sheets off, got cold, pulled them back on. Startled at every unfamiliar creak and groan, and every time she looked at the shadows in the corner, she couldn't quite figure out what was making them.

Mostly, she was royally pissed off.

Seventh grade was terrifying enough, but getting yanked out of Rosenberg Middle only a few weeks into the school year, then dragged across like six states to start ALL OVER somewhere else? Practically kidnapping. She'd googled CPS to see if they could do anything but ultimately never called, too worried they'd laugh at her.

Oh, your parents want to MOVE? *We've got kids with* REAL *problems, dummy.*

The prospect of starting a new school scared her. At least at Rosenberg she'd had her best friend, Gracia. Two days before, standing in Gracia's driveway, they'd promised to keep in touch, to be best friends forever—they'd even created a super-complicated plan for how they could go to junior prom, still four years away. Then on the way home, Damien had wrapped his hand in hers and leaned his head on her shoulder—Mom busy singing along to a Taylor Swift song on the radio—she'd realized her whole life in Columbus was dead, deader than her fifth grade class' hamster, Michaela.

She'd cried for DAYS when the class voted to give the hamster the same name as her, and her stupid teacher Mrs. Freeling called it a good lesson in democracy, whatever that meant. She'd spent untold hours staring into the mirror, wondering if her upturned nose and disturbingly small chin were actually rodent-like, or if the kids were being cruel for unknown, childish reasons.

Maybe a little of both.

Once the other Michaela died, thanks to a garlic clove stealthily dropped into her cage, the other kids seemed to forget the episode completely and became her friends again.

Except for Daryl, who wore a black armband every day for the rest of the year and broke into uncontrollable weeping every time Mrs. Freeling called on the REAL Michaela, but he was weird and nobody liked him anyway.

"This sucks," Michaela hissed.

"It's not so bad," Damien said softly from the doorway.

Michaela stifled a yelp and lunged, grabbing her little brother and tickling him.

He HATED that.

Damien squirmed, writhing in her grasp. "Stop."

Michaela let him go. He wiped his ear with the hem of his shirt, shooting her filthy looks.

"Brought it on yourself," Michaela said.

Damien huffed, sat down in her desk chair. "How do you feel about all this, anyway?"

"The move?"

"Mm."

A question neither mother nor father had bothered to ask. She bit her lip. "Sucks."

Damien nodded quickly. "No one asked you, right?"

"What do you want, Damien?"

Damien stood, stretching his thin bones. "Just checking up on my big sister."

"I'm not an idiot."

"Fair enough. You heard Sabrina, earlier. I'm thinking we can...use this."

"How?"

"She's already got herself all twisted around. I've been playing with her for years. But now? We can do something. Something BIG."

Michaela worried at the comforter. "I don't think—"

"With all due respect, dear sister," Damien said, Cheshire grin stretching his face, "THAT is my department."

So it began.

Damien and Michaela left for the bus stop, and Sabrina's pulse immediately ratcheted up several notches. Usually it was a relief—she could resort to being Sabrina rather than Mom. Not now. Part of her wanted to run to the bus stop, drag them both back home. For years, she CRAVED alone time. Now?

She still wasn't alone.

She wished she could go back to those busy, buzzy moments before her trip to the basement. Before all the promise the beautiful new house contained had been tainted with horror.

But she couldn't.

Sabrina put the chair back against the basement door, just in case, then went into the kitchen and made herself some tea. She preferred coffee, but needed something to calm her nerves, not rattle them. Even so, the screaming of the teapot nearly made her jump through the window.

After, she sat at the kitchen table, sipping a stale and unsatisfying packet of chamomile, hyper-vigilant.

She sorely needed sleep. Had precious little the night before, waking every time she drifted off. Late, very late, she'd finally fallen asleep, only to suffer from the most horrible dreams. She couldn't remember a single one, only the way they made her feel.

Awful.

Hal, for his part, had been supportive if skeptical. Offered to let her drive him to work so she could keep the car, but she declined. What was the point? If they were going to continue living in the house on James Circle—and unless Hal got an even better job offer somewhere else they wouldn't be moving any time soon—she had to make her peace with it. She couldn't walk around jumping at shadows in her own house, she'd go crazy, become one of those women who drowned her own children in the bathtub or drove her car into the lake.

Once her car arrived. Whenever that might be.

MAN, FUCK THIS HOUSE

Sabrina reached for her mug, tea spilling over the rim. Were her hands really shaking that badly? She sipped—too hot—put it back down. Drummed her fingers lightly on the edge of the saucer. She really needed to compose a to-do list, there were a never-ending number of things she needed to do, but she couldn't concentrate. She kept looking from one doorway to another, cocking her head to listen for sounds she'd only thought she heard.

Maybe if she turned on the TV, that would help. A little ambient sound to disguise any noises the house made, natural or otherwise. She went into the living room, flipped on the TV. Static roared through the speakers, nothing but snow on the screen—she'd forgotten, neither cable nor internet were hooked up yet. When was the cable guy coming?

She couldn't remember.

She went into the kitchen, grabbed the magnetic whiteboard off the fridge, and sat down to compose that deferred to-do list. Their communal laundry basket in the upstairs closet was already overflowing—after two days—but no, she had more stuff to put away and organize, pictures to hang, furniture placement decisions she wanted to revisit.

Or, she could take a bath.

Play some relaxing music on her phone, light a few candles, slip into a warm bubbly broth and lose herself for a few moments. She could already feel her heartbeat slowing back to something resembling its resting rate.

Leaving her tea mostly untouched, Sabrina headed upstairs. The chair was still jammed under the basement doorknob, right where she left it, and that made her feel better. Perhaps she'd imagined things, OR maybe only the basement was haunted. She could live with that, right? Make Hal do the laundry, he wasn't some clueless detergent commercial husband who'd drink bleach before he ever used it on his whites. Hell, he wouldn't even mind, he often tried to do little things around the house. SHE chased HIM off—downright territorial with the Swiffer.

As she passed the basement door, the knob jiggled.

Sabrina froze, one foot raised.

Oh no.

She stared at the knob, but it didn't move again. It HAD moved, though. Hadn't it? If she could imagine a large man toting her boxes down the basement steps, she could certainly imagine a doorknob twisting of its own accord, couldn't she?

Or.

Carefully, Sabrina took a single step back.

The doorknob jiggled again.

Stepped forward—nothing.

Stepped back.

Jiggle.

She giggled, like she was back in college at a frat party, tipsy on wine coolers. GIGGLED. And then laughed, stomping on the board in question, making the doorknob jiggle over and over and over again.

It's an old house, what do you expect?

Sabrina wiped tears from her eyes, shaking her head at her own silliness. Not that this explained everything—no amount of creaky boards could manifest a large, box-moving, disappearing man—but this one thing, this single rational explanation, lifted the weight off her shoulders. The laughter, the release, was exactly what she needed. She felt at home in her new house in a way she'd not since they moved in.

She left the chair in its place, though. Until she figured out what was going on with the basement, or a sufficient amount of time had passed for her to discount the memory entirely, she wasn't QUITE ready to leave the door unsecured.

Still.

Sabrina headed upstairs—maybe not bounding per se, but definitely with a newfound spring in her step, head nearly spinning with thoughts of a hot, bubbly bath, and all the delicious decadence it promised. She pushed open the bedroom door, registering the light on in the bathroom.

Hal must have left it on, she thought. He'd been the last one in the bathroom?

Right?

The second she stepped into the bathroom, she knew that wasn't true. Hal hadn't been the last person in the master suite after all.

If he had, the bathwater in the tub would have gone cold a long time ago.

Damien wasn't looking forward to junior high—grad school seemed much more his speed—but the one thing that seemed to recommend it over elementary was the ease with which middle schoolers could skip class.

Or so he imagined.

It HAD to be at least a little easier, though—changing classrooms five times a day gave one the opportunity to disappear, whereas sitting in Mr. Tuthill's sixth grade class did not. Tuthill himself was giving a staggeringly ahistorical lesson on the battle of Thermopylae, grounded more in Zack Snyder's highly-stylized *300* than any historical record.

Damien snapped three pencils fighting the urge to correct him.

"Zerf-zees had millions of troops, giant elephants, actual MONSTERS," Tuthill said, drawing some sort of lobster/human hybrid on the board. "But, I'll let you in on a little secret, kids." Tuthill turned from the board, chalk in hand, an erection obscenely pushing out at the twenty-seven children in his class. "It's not the size of the army. It's all about the warrior mentality. See, when I was in the National Guard—"

Damien's hand shot up, almost of its own free will. "Mr. Tuthill?"

Tuthill blinked. "Yes, uh, new kid?"

"May I use the restroom?"

"Don't you wanna know who won?"

Damien smiled diplomatically. "It's sort of... urgent."

"All right, spoiler alert! The Persians defeated Leonightus' army, but only because this blasted *gimp*—"

Damien cringed at the cruel and offensive description of Ephialtes, who might have been a traitor but didn't deserve such an ableist epithet.

Tuthill continued bellowing, babbling, working up a sweat, before eventually wearing himself out, his lank brown hair plastered to his forehead, pit stains spreading beneath his short sleeve button-up.

He FINALLY grabbed the hall pass from his desk and handed it to Damien. "Give 'em hell, son."

Damien resisted the urge to salute him, instead said a quick thank you, and headed for the bathroom. Unlike his old school in Columbus, Hooper actually put doors on the stalls. Damien appreciated the smidgeon of dignity the gesture conveyed. Previously, he'd have to carefully schedule his bowel movements, or in a pinch fake an illness so he could use the bathroom in the nurse's office so as not to make poo-poo so exposed.

Here, he could finally get a little time to himself.

Nature wasn't even calling at the moment. No, he was driven by a far more pressing urge, to get away from the dizzardly Mr. Tuthill before he did something that would truly confirm Sabrina's suspicions vis a vis his supposed demonic/sociopathic aspect.

But also, he wanted to check in with Michaela, make sure they were still on for after school.

Damien sent her a quick text—*how's ur day going?* He thought about sitting down, but didn't want to sully his trousers on the surely cooties-infested seat.

His phone pinged. Damien smiled—he'd gotten lucky, maybe she'd gotten sick of her idiot teachers and taken a powder as well—and opened the message.

Shouldn't you be in school?

Same unknown phone number. Same overly-familiar tone.

Damien scowled at the phone. Whoever this was, they weren't funny.

Ignoring the urge to send a rejoinder—undoubtedly far more incisive than anything the mystery texter could imagine—Damien simply blocked the number.

He admired the graffiti on the inside of the bathroom door—some very uncharitable but likely-true things were said about Mr. Tuthill, with panache—and waited for Michaela to reply. Could be a moment, she'd likely have to sneak out of class herself.

His phone beeped. Another text from the mystery number he'd just blocked.

You're not getting rid of me that easy.

Sabrina woke up face-down on the bathroom floor.

She blinked, the tile cold against her cheek. She pushed herself up into a seated position, trying to figure out how she'd gotten there, or how she'd ended up on the FLOOR of all places. None of it made sense. She looked around, hoping for some clue to explain her predicament.

Nothing other than the fogged-up window.

A wave of exhaustion roiled over her. Sabrina felt faint, so she leaned against the bathtub.

THE BATHTUB.

Everything came rushing back—her unwanted morning tea, the curious step that made the basement doorknob jiggle, her luxurious decision to defer household chores in favor of a long, relaxing—

BATH.

She'd come upstairs, intending to draw herself a

bath, only to find the tub already filled. And recently, too, it wasn't merely some silently useless romantic gesture on Hal's part for her to find after he'd already headed off to work. No, the water had been hot to the touch.

Not warm, luke or otherwise.

Piping hot.

Now she peered into the tub, hoping to confirm her suspicions—or not, as the case might be. The tub was empty, but a flufference of bubbles around the drain marked this as a new development. She hadn't imagined a thing. Someone had filled the tub for her.

The house drew me a bath. HAD

The thought popped into Sabrina's mind unbidden, but it seemed right. Not to mention the only possibility, unless someone had broken in—

Now THAT seemed to make even more sense. The same man who'd carried the box down to the basement? How closely had she inspected the crawlspace, anyway? Maybe he slipped into some hidey-hole, some hidden passageway, wriggling off into the earth? Living in a secret alcove, an unofficial and unseen resident of the house?

Maybe he was watching her RIGHT NOW.

Sabrina gasped, looked about for a weapon. The bathroom offered nothing obvious, because it was a bathroom, not an armory. A man that big would simply laugh if she tried to brain him with a shampoo bottle or a bar of soap. Wait, the towel rack—

Something creaked out beyond the bedroom door—a long, slow noise, like someone, perhaps a very large man, leaning forward to peek around the doorframe.

Sabrina slammed the bathroom door shut, flipping the lock. The door was too flimsy to stand against a concentrated assault from the basement dweller, but it might give her time to, to—do what exactly?

Call 911.

Sabrina's heart dropped into her stomach as she reached for her pocket, hoping she hadn't forgotten her phone downstairs. *Thank God*—she pulled out her phone, thumb fumbling across the screen, somehow managed to dial.

The call took an interminable amount of time to connect, but then:

"911, what is your emergency?"

Sabrina nearly fainted a second time from sheer relief.

The police officer—a heavyset bald man who looked like a shelled turtle but had a calm, attentive demeanor—scoured every inch of the house, from the front door to the basement, the children's rooms, the kitchen, the master bedroom, bathroom and all.

And found precisely nothing.

Sabrina accompanied him downstairs, showed him the crawlspace. He thoroughly inspected it with his Mag-Lite, combing every inch for hidden apertures and finding nothing but a rat-hole.

"Why didn't you call us the first time, ma'am?" he asked, tapping the side of the rathole with his flashlight.

Sabrina looked down at her house-slippers. "I didn't think anyone'd believe me."

MAN, FUCK THIS HOUSE

"I understand, ma'am," he said quietly, then suggested they go upstairs.

After touring the rest of the house, they took a seat in the living room. Sabrina offered him one of Zephyr's sandwiches, but he declined.

"Watching my carbs," he said, patting his stomach. "Now, a couple things." He drew a small, spiral-bound notebook from his pocket, but merely gestured with it. "I'd change all the locks. Never know who's got a copy of the key when you buy a new place. Also think about getting a security system. My brother's got a firm, best in Jackson Hill. I can get you his card if you want."

Sabrina nodded, it couldn't hurt.

"Now, we checked the crawlspace, and even though things couldn't have gone down the way you told me, the mind does funny things in times of stress. Entirely possible you did have an intruder, and he went back up the stairs."

"Maybe?" Sabrina could clearly picture the man climbing into the crawlspace, she didn't think she'd imagined it, but that explanation made a little more sense. Maybe she had gotten turned around, somehow.

"You said he touched a box?" the cop asked.

"That's right."

The cop put the notebook back in his pocket. "I can dust for fingerprints. Maybe something comes back, maybe it doesn't."

"But I touched the box," Sabrina said. "Maybe Hal, the kids, the movers—"

The cop shrugged. "Not saying we'll find anything, but if this guy did break into your house, he might be in the system. Who knows?"

"Okay."

The cop went out to his cruiser, then back downstairs. He managed to smear fingerprint powder everywhere, but after a few minutes he declared he'd found some useable prints. "Probably be a week or two, but I'll let you know—"

Footsteps echoed across the ceiling. Heavy.

The cop drew his gun, motioning for Sabrina to get behind him. He trained his weapon on the stairs. Sabrina disappeared into a corner, trying to make herself tiny, disappear behind the washer.

But secretly elated someone else was about to see exactly what she had.

The top step creaked. The cop sighted down his pistol, free hand reaching for his radio.

"You on the stairs, don't move!"

Silence, air pressurized like before a thunderstorm.

Then—"Sabrina? Hun?"

Sabrina looked up at the stairs.

Hal stood at the top, briefcase in one hand, a bouquet of flowers in the other, and a very confused look on his—thankfully still intact—face.

"That ain't him, right?" the cop said, already lowering his gun.

Sabrina couldn't quite manage a sigh of relief. "No."

A block from the corner of Allen and Flanagan, Damien pulled the cord. Air brakes hissed, the bus rolled to a stop.

MAN, FUCK THIS HOUSE

Beside him, Michaela looked up from her phone. "Still can't believe you talked me into this. Better be worth the bus fare."

Damien flashed his special smile, the one reserved just for her. "When have I ever steered you wrong?"

Michaela arched an eyebrow. "Last Fourth of July?"

"Other than that."

"The Columbus County Fair?"

"Oh please, cotton candy is essentially inedible anyway."

She leaned in, lowering her voice. "Disney. World."

Damien blinked. His sister *did* have a point.

"You getting off or what?" the bus driver asked.

"Coming!" Damien cried, springing from his seat. He practically dragged Michaela down the aisle, dodging the metal feet of elderly peoples' walkers and the actual feet of equally-elderly people who didn't yet need them, almost kicking over a plastic grocery bag filled with oranges—no, they were the small ones, Cuties—and finally down the steps.

"Thank you for your service," Damien called over his shoulder, but the accordion door had already slammed shut.

No matter, they'd arrived at their destination, a slick, modern shopping center anchored by Ralphs grocery, bookended by drug stores and nail salons, but most importantly featuring Jackson Hill's sole—

"Forever 31," Michaela said, breathlessly, their seconds-ago argument about Damien's plan and her money already forgotten.

The Halloween store, a seasonal pop-up chain that

took over abandoned storefronts and filled them with death, sat directly beside Ralphs. A fifteen-foot tall inflatable reaper beckoned, scythe waving in the wind, while all manner of vampires, werewolves, and pumpkin-headed axe murderers stalked the sidewalk.

"Let's go," Damien said.

They crossed the parking lot, the reaper looming larger, the sound of the motor humming louder, a mesmeric drone that glazed their eyes and slacked their jaws. Even Damien, who normally scoffed at spooks and shadows, felt a tingle of excitement lance through his body.

And not just because he planned to shoplift some mallocreme pumpkins.

The automatic doors whooshed open. They entered, minds bedazzled by the arrays of blinking lights, the rows upon rows of decorations, costumes, and makeup. Fall scents filled the air—aerosolized pumpkin spice, apple cinnamon, browning leaves.

"Melp 'oo?" asked a tall woman wearing a zombified elk head and a nametag reading *Shaney*.

"What?"

The woman pulled her mask off, looking flushed and sweaty. "Sorry, hard to breathe in that thing. Can I help you?"

"Just browsing," Damien said quickly. "Come on, sis."

Michaela seemed entranced by a pair of talking gargoyles, so Damien yanked her sleeve. "We really need to figure out our costumes this year."

"Not now, we're on a mission." She had a point, though. The Haskins siblings had a long-standing Halloween tradition of wearing matching outfits. Over the years they'd been Sid and Nancy, Ronald and Nancy, Jeff Gillooly and Nancy—Damien enjoyed that latter one because he got to wear a sparkly figure-skating outfit, and everyone at school looked appropriately horrified when a ski-masked and mustachioed Michaela rushed out of the locker room and pretend-smashed him in the knee with a telescoping baton. The only problem was keeping their Halloween shenanigans—that word always made Damien giggle—secret from their parents, particularly Sabrina. Damien usually spent the earlier part of Halloween Eve standing silently in the corner or whispering creepy things to Sabrina like *they're here* before sneaking out to go trick-or-treating with his sister.

"What about Nancy Pelosi and Mitch McConnell?" Michaela asked, pausing in front of a rack of truly-terrifying political masks.

Damien cringed. "Can't I go as someone who ISN'T named Nancy this year?"

"Why?"

"We're running out of Nancies. They're not the most notable people."

Michaela's eyebrows knitted together briefly, then she smiled. "We haven't done Nancy Grace and Casey Anthony!"

"Will there be a blood-drenched baby doll involved?"

"Duh."

Damien stuck out his pinkie. "Deal." Michaela shook it. "Now, let's not forget why we're here."

They headed off down the aisles. Damien knew exactly what he needed to take his lifelong practical joke on his mother to the next level.

The costume blood was a problem—none of it smelled enough like actual blood for his taste—but they really did make some astoundingly realistic prosthetics these days, and Damien figured he could cross the blood bridge when they got there.

After all, practically everyone he knew was full of the stuff.

They were standing in the checkout line, waiting for a beleaguered mother of triplets to buy three Spider-Man costumes, when Michaela's phone rang. She ignored it. A minute later Damien's went off too.

"Father," he said, holding up his phone so she could see it. Odd. Hal rarely called, Sabrina was the family's communications director.

The triplet mom completed her triple-Spidey purchase, and the clerk—Shaney from earlier, off the floor and no longer wearing her too-hot mask—motioned them forward.

That's when the *911* texts began.

At dinner, Hal couldn't leave it alone.

Sabrina kept her gaze leveled down at her plate—a hastily-cobbled together mishmash of Zephyr's sandwiches, plus baked potato—and didn't say much, pushing her food from one quadrant to the other. Hal wasn't mad, per se, but was making far more of the incident than he needed to, turning it into something between a near-death experience and a joke.

At her expense, of course.

"I thought that cop was gonna—" Hal sighted

down his butter knife, pretended to blow holes in the fridge. "Bam! Bam! Bam!"

Michaela giggled, then tensed, putting a hand over her mouth and looking at Sabrina.

Damien, predictably, said nothing.

Hal tried to spin the butter knife like an old west gunfighter, but it went sailing end over end, bouncing off the cabinets. He offered the table a bemused grin— *Wyatt Earp I'm not, kids*—and got himself a new knife from the drawer.

You weren't using the first one, Sabrina thought, annoyed he was making more work for her, but didn't say anything. After all, she could just slip the knife back in the silverware if she wanted, no one would notice.

"So," Hal said, laying his new butter knife at the top of his plate, "your mom thinks the house is haunted."

"Hal!"

He winked at the kids, doing his worst *Father Knows Best* impression. "Hun, it's fine. We don't keep secrets in this house, do we?"

"No," Michaela said, her face spasming so badly she looked like she might fall out of her chair.

"That's right," Hal said, nodding to himself. "We're a team. Back when I led the Truffle Hogs to the State Championship—"

Semi-finals, Sabrina silently corrected.

"—if I kept the playbook to myself, the wide receivers wouldn't know what routes to run, now would they?"

The reference was effectively lost on every single person in the room. Michaela played softball, Damien nothing at all, and sports had never interested Sabrina much—just a reason for men to get even drunker than they usually did and scream their feelings.

"They sure wouldn't, daddio," Michaela said, nodding vigorously. She'd started doing this in the last year, this knowing, exaggerated faux-daddy's girl act.

It pissed Sabrina off to no end.

"That's right, monkey," Hal said.

This time, Michaela ignored the use of her most-hated nickname, further confirming she was in the middle of a performance. The purpose of which, Sabrina suspected, was simply to push and pull on the power dynamics of the Haskins household, sowing tween girl chaos for its own sake.

Too bad boarding school wasn't a thing anymore, or at least a thing within the squarely middle-class Haskins bubble, because Sabrina didn't relish the prospect of being trapped in a house with either of her soon-to-be pubescing spawn—Michaela playing these power games, and Damien might just hack them all to bits with an axe when his little body grew from boy to near-man.

"Anyway," Hal said, "we're a team, is the point. Team Haskins. So, what do you think, kids? Is the house haunted?"

"Pssh, as if," Michaela said, but without malice.

"Yes," Damien intoned, blankly.

Everyone turned to look at him—Damien speaking at dinner was a rare occasion, not unlike Hailey's comet passing by in the night.

"Why makes you say that, buddy?" Hal asked.

MAN, FUCK THIS HOUSE

"Have you seen a g-g-g-ghost?" He Scooby-Dooed his voice, punctuating the sentence with a full-body shiver.

Damien shook his head—one slow, deliberate side-to-side swivel. Sabrina could almost hear the hinges in his neck squeak.

"Well, what then, bud? Why do you think the house is haunted?"

Sabrina leaned forward in her chair. As much as her youngest frightened her, perhaps if she was right about him—spawned from Satan's seed rather than Hal's—he could tell her what was going on. Who the big, burly man was, why a bath had been drawn for her.

Maybe, just maybe, he'd be on *her* side.

Damien looked from his father, to his sister, to her, expression never changing. Peering deep into Sabrina's eyes, Damien said, library-quiet, "Because they're hungry."

Hal blinked. "Hungry? What's that mean, pal?"

Damien took half a sandwich from his plate. He walked over to the wall beside the refrigerator—blank and pale blue. He turned back to the family, all staring at him with rapt attention.

Especially Sabrina.

"It means," Damien said, "they must be fed." He held out the half-sandwich to the empty spot on the wall. One second, it was in his little, ten-year-old hand.

The next second?

It wasn't.

Sabrina lay in bed, pretending to scroll Instagram. Hal next to her, engrossed in another Baldacci book. She envied Hal's ability to read so quickly. He had a different book in his hand practically every time she saw him.

Something hadn't agreed with Hal, dinner-wise, because he kept grunting and rubbing his stomach, a slight gurgle audible through the comforter.

Dinner hadn't agreed with Sabrina, either, even though her stomach felt fine. She kept replaying the scene in her head, over and over again—Damien walking to that utterly unremarkable spot on the wall, holding out his half-sandwich.

Then poof.

Gone.

She'd screamed, rushed at her son. Grabbed his little stick-arms so hard her hands left wicked red marks in his forearms, just below the elbow. Shook him, demanding he tell her what he knew, until Hal pulled her away.

"Sabrina! Stop it, stop it!" Hal repeated, but she wouldn't stop it, couldn't stop it. She'd just seen a GHOST eat a SANDWICH, for Pete's sake. The supernatural was real, and hungry, and on more than nodding terms with her creepy little kid.

Eventually Hal muscled her into the living room and took the kids to bed. They didn't talk about what happened, and after—Sabrina wasn't sure how long, the minutes didn't so much blur together as slip by unnoticed—they went to bed, her trailing him up the stairs, neither touching each other. The dishes in the sink nagged at her, but they'd keep. They brushed their teeth at the his and hers sinks, changed, climbed into bed, a healthy couple inches between them.

"Hrrm," Hal muttered, shifting from one side to the other.

Sabrina exited out of Instagram—she couldn't bear to look at any more of the dumb fitness mommy accounts she followed, they always felt like some cheap, tawdry form of self-abuse. Logic-brain knew the washboard abs poking out of tiny lycra shorts, the perfectly-coiffed kids invariably named Scout or Topher or Hunter, the family photo-ops at their personal CrossFit gym in the backyard next to their infinity pool, all of it was a put-on, some carefully-conjured alternate reality. A blink, a flash, a millisecond of perfection in a lifetime of dirty diapers, upended cereal bowls, crayon portraits all over the walls. How she would have loved to have a single moment as perfect as any of the dozens of photos the monstrous mommy-models added to their feeds every day.

Instead, she was stuck with all the *other* moments.

She shot a glance over at Hal—still nose-in-book, but a fraught expression on his face—and debated for the millionth time what to say. Even though he'd seen exactly what she had, it didn't even seem to register. Everything she'd experienced had gone from a joke to a liability in his eyes. How much longer would he entertain her paranoid delusions?

They're not.

Were they?

Enough. She had to know. Had to ask.

"Hal?"

He groaned lightly, fumbled for his bookmark. Looked over at her, not even feigning interest. "Yeah?"

"You're okay, right?"

"Just a little indigestion."

"Okay." That took all of four seconds. She swallowed, steeling herself. "Tonight, before—before I—" she was chewing her cheek into hamburger, "—you saw that too, right? The sandwich?"

He set the book on the nightstand. Took off his glasses, folding them carefully, placed them alongside the book. Stared off into the distance for a long moment, evidently considering his words. "Hun, I'm not sure how to say this, so I'll just come out with it. Do you hate our son?"

The words hit her like a slap across the face. "How could you say that?"

"I'm not blind. I know how hard the pregnancy was for you, the post-partum. You've never really been the same since."

"Hal, I—"

"I emailed my boss earlier. Told him I'm working from home tomorrow. Also looked up some specialists. They've got some very good therapists, right here in Jackson Hill. Figure I'll make some calls, see if I can get you in to talk to somebody."

Sabrina leaned back into the pillows, folding her arms tightly across her chest. "You think I'm crazy."

"No, hun. I think—I think the move's been hard on you, but it's not just that. I've seen you with him. Damien. There's always been this, this distance. Er." He scooted towards the edge of the bed. "I'm just saying, it wouldn't hurt to have someone to talk to. Get it all out, you know?"

"Get it all out." Part of her wanted to toss the covers off, grab her pillow, go sleep on the couch.

But then she'd be closer to the basement. And the spot on the kitchen wall.

"Just think about it, all I'm saying. Uh." Hal got up and went into the bathroom. A beat later, the sound of running water came through the door, and Sabrina shivered, thinking about the bath that drew itself.

Eventually he came back in, lay down. She turned away, clutching her pillow tightly.

After a long moment, she said, "Tell me you saw the sandwich, Hal."

A light snore was the only response.

Sleep was a long time coming for Sabrina Haskins. Again.

Damien's phone beeped.

Michaela: *Downstairs. Now.*

Damien threw off the covers, hurriedly changed out of his SpongeBob PJs—a private, childish affectation he'd yet to shed and would be mortified if anyone ever discovered—and donned a simple silk robe instead, dark blue with a very grown-up wooden ship emblazoned over the breast pocket. He opened his bedroom door quietly and padded down the stairs. A step creaked beneath his feet, he nearly cursed under his breath—he hadn't fully cataloged the house's noisy spots, something he very much needed to understand if he were to succeed in his current endeavors.

Michaela waited in the dining room, seated at the long, formal table the family never used, preferring the more casual round table in the kitchen instead. Her arms were crossed, hair up in a ponytail.

Meaning she meant business.

"Sit," Michaela said quietly.

Damien gave her a curt nod, pulled out a chair across from her. Motioned for her to speak her piece.

"The sandwich thing," she said without preamble.

"Yes?"

Michaela leaned across the table. "It's too much, Damien! You shouldn't have done that."

That was what he'd been pulled out of bed for? His dinner table sleight of hand? Sabrina had reacted poorly, sure, but Damien had been quite proud of himself. A flick of the wrist and the half-sandwich disappeared down his sleeve. Granted he'd garnered some nasty stains on the inside of his shirt from whatever near-gruel their hippie neighbor slathered over the bread, but still.

Worth it.

Damien scoffed. "If the woman can't recognize a rudimentary parlor trick for what it is, she doesn't deserve to be sane."

Michaela rolled her eyes. "You can see it, can't you? She's—she's not *right*."

"When has she ever been?"

"I—"

"Wait, don't answer that. I know precisely when she was last *right*. The day before I was born. You had two years of normalcy. Two years of motherhood, followed by ten of something I'd consider close enough for government work. We should all be so lucky."

Michaela drew her feet up under her, fussing with the sleeves of her hoodie. "You know what I mean. Ever since we moved, she's been, I don't know, edgy. This whole thing about the house being haunted?"

"Which *you* believe."

"I do not."

"Please," Damien said. "Admit you're open to the idea, at least."

A long, long moment stretched out between them, then—small, soft: "Yes."

"Nothing to be ashamed of," Damien said, leaning in himself now. "Lots of—" he almost said children, "—people believe in the supernatural. It's not real, obviously, but it's...fun. Like our trip to the Halloween store earlier."

"Do you have to be so condescending?"

If you don't care for the message, disparage the delivery.

"If you're waiting for me to apologize, you'll be sitting in that chair until your skin shrivels to parchment."

Michaela slapped the table, a loud report that echoed off the walls and made Damien fear she'd wake their parents. "Just stop, okay? It's not about that. It's about Mom. She's not well, and you're making it worse. It was all fun and games until we moved into this house, but now?"

"What?"

"I don't know." Michaela slumped over the table, drawing her hoodie up over her hair. Becoming a faceless shade. "All I know is, you need to lay off, Damien. Stop messing with Mom."

"I won't."

"Then I'll tell."

"You wouldn't."

Michaela's nails clattered across the table. "I would." She drew herself up in her chair. "I will."

Silence hung in the air. Damian looked down at his own nails—direly in need of a trim—and considered his options. Lie to Michaela, his only confidante? Or abandon his life's project?

Neither option seemed palatable.

"Tell them *what*, exactly?" he finally said.

Michaela blinked. "What?"

"I said, what are you going to tell them? That I've been pretending to be a demonic little imp? That I'm—" Damien sighed, "—a perilously normal child, albeit an extraordinarily intelligent one? What will that accomplish? You cannot disabuse Sabrina of her beliefs, and Father? I've never met a more oblivious life form, let alone *human*, in my ten years on this planet. He sees nothing, knows nothing. I'd bet body parts he has no internal monologue whatsoever."

"But—it's *Dad*."

"How many times have we mocked the idiots of the world? Are you really so surprised to find your own father counted amongst their number?"

Michaela retreated into her hoodie. "You're really awful sometimes, you know that?"

Damien stood, abruptly. "You sound just like Sabrina. You. Know. That?"

The dam burst, Michaela threw her head down on the dining room table, sobbing.

MAN, FUCK THIS HOUSE

Damien walked around the table, headed back to his beloved SpongeBob pajamas and bed. He bent down and whispered in his sister's ear, "Stay out of my way."

Michaela made a noise that might've been *bastard,* or might've been nothing at all.

Either way, her histrionics changed nothing. Her participation in the plan had always been optional.

Just like her continued existence.

WEDNESDAY

SABRINA BARELY SLEPT. She dozed off shortly in the small hours, only to snap awake again once the earliest rays of dawn filtered through the blinds. Hal still snored next to her, turned away, on top of the sheet.

She turned off the alarm on her phone before it rang and went downstairs. At the landing, sweat broke out on her brow. She crept through the lower level of her own house, peeking around corners, fearful something might pop out to consume her like the sandwich.

She intended to brew coffee, the first step in the complex morning ritual required to keep the Haskins family operational, but when she stepped into the kitchen she froze.

The coffeepot was full.

Fresh, too—the air thick with the scent of warm java. She looked over her shoulder, then advanced into the kitchen, step by excruciating step, focused on the wooden knife block on the counter.

Maybe she couldn't cut a ghost, but she'd surely try, if the opportunity presented itself.

She reached the counter, pulled a knife from the block. Realized she'd grabbed a bread knife, unlikely to intimidate anyone, corporeal or ethereal. Pulled another, a nasty-looking butcher knife.

Back to the counter, Sabrina raised the knife in what she hoped was a menacing manner and hissed, "Where are you?"

Nothing.

No specters emerged to challenge her, no ghosts nor goblins poked their heads out of the cracks and crevices in the walls. Just a woman, bangs plastered to her forehead, threatening the air with a knife over a fresh pot of coffee.

Absurd.

Laughter bubbled up from her guts, tears poured from her eyes. She doubled over, dropping the knife, the clatter resounding off the walls.

"Hun?"

Hal stood in the doorway—bathrobed, hair mussed, a handful of strands sticking up in a cowlick.

Sabrina stopped laughing, wiped tears from her eyes. Tried to compose her features into something resembling a serious expression. "I dropped the knife," she said lamely, pointing at the butcher knife on the tile.

"You dropped the knife."

Sabrina nodded quickly. "Silly, it just slipped out of my hand. Almost took a toe off." She lifted her foot, wiggled her toes.

Hal made a point of looking at his watch. "Doctor should be open soon." He frowned and walked away, mumbling to himself.

Great.

Not for the first time, Sabrina asked herself if she was going insane. A pointless question—how would one know? If you had the good sense to *ask* if you were going crazy, you couldn't be.

Right?

She stooped, knees groaning, picked up the knife. Slid it back into its home.

It'd already done enough damage.

The rest of the morning passed agonizingly slowly.

Sabrina thought she'd be glad to have Hal home, but that wasn't the case. He took over the dining room, turning it into a makeshift office, and while she didn't begrudge him the space, no matter where she went she could *feel* him down there.

Nominally working.

Mostly judging.

It was weird. They rarely quarreled, because there was so little to quarrel about. Hal picked up after himself, mostly. Brought home a decent paycheck. Bought her flowers. They still had sex—just the other night, even.

Now Sabrina couldn't imagine touching him.

She kept thinking about that moment in the kitchen, the sandwich disappearing out of her strange little son's hand. Where could it have gone? And why was Hal fixated on her reaction, instead of the impossibility he'd witnessed?

Sabrina grabbed a basket of laundry and headed down to the basement, hoping the large man would make an appearance again, and she'd scream and Hal would come running and he'd *see,* he'd *see,* and then she wouldn't be so alone.

Other than a brief moment when she thought they were out of detergent—just enough for a single load—

nothing remotely frightening happened in the basement. After, she puttered around the house, avoiding the dining room. Hal called her in, once, telling her he'd scheduled an appointment with a Dr. Sanderson for three weeks hence—he said that last part with an uncommon bitterness—and went back to his work.

By lunchtime, Sabrina had had her fill. She had to go somewhere, get away from the house, the husband, all of it. But her car STILL hadn't arrived, and she wasn't about to ask Hal to borrow the Camry—he'd probably think she'd drive it off a cliff in her current state.

That's when she remembered the plate.

The neighbor's plate, which needed returning. A minor errand, to be sure. But it'd get her out of the house, at least.

Sabrina went to the sink—the plate gleamed in the dish rack. The spooks hadn't only made coffee, apparently. She wasn't sure whether to be grateful or afraid or angry. A strange admixture of all three boiled in her veins.

Maybe THAT was worst of all—she never quite knew how to feel.

Sabrina picked up the dish, about to stick her head into the dining room to tell Hal she was leaving, but stopped. Why should she check in with him? Sabrina left—shutting the door quietly—and headed across the street to Zephyr's. The front door opened the minute she stepped foot on the sidewalk, the older lady coming out onto the porch wrapped in a ratty-yet-inviting cardigan—the same yellow hue as her house predominated—a mug in one hand, a bemused expression on her face.

MAN, FUCK THIS HOUSE

"I was wondering where my favorite plate was."

"Sorry, we just finished the sandwiches." Sabrina stopped short of the porch. "This is your favorite plate?"

Zephyr took the plate from her. "I tell that to all my dinnerware. Shh."

"Oh." Sabrina stood there awkwardly. "The sandwiches were delicious, by the way. Very kind of you."

"Just being neighborly. Would you like to come in for a chugacchino?" She hefted the mug.

Sabrina had no idea what that was, but relished the thought of being inside someone else's presumably non-haunted house. "Sure."

"Well, come on then." Zephyr turned, disappearing into the house.

Sabrina mounted the steps, let herself in the front door. The heavy scent of incense nearly bowled her over. Zephyr's living room matched her personality. *Bohemian* would easily cover it—tapestries on the walls, tribal-looking masks and knickknacks, decorations woven out of rope. A spinning wheel occupied one corner, reminding her of *Rumpelstiltskin,* while an upright piano sat beneath a colorful mural of trumpet-blowing jazz musicians.

"Make yourself at home," Zephyr called from the kitchen.

Sabrina moved some throw pillows out of the way and settled onto the big, overstuffed couch. She shifted around, trying to get comfortable—less out of actual discomfort than because she didn't have a phone to occupy her.

Zephyr came out of the kitchen carrying two

mugs. She handed one to Sabrina. "Ever had a chugaccino?"

Sabrina peered into the mug—looked like coffee. Which made her heart beat a little faster.

"What is it?"

"Mushroom coffee." Zephyr plopped down next to Sabrina. "Not the fun kind, I'm afraid."

"Oh." Sabrina blew on her drink until the steam dissipated, took a sip. A little earthy, but in the same zip code as actual java. "It's good."

"And good for you. Know what goes really well with it?"

"No?"

Zephyr opened a small wooden box on the coffee table, revealing a stash of hand-rolled joints. She took one from the box and stuck it between her lips. "Munt 'ome?"

Sabrina hadn't touched weed since college, and only then a handful of times—it either didn't work for her, or left her incapacitated, burrowing into the closest couch she could find.

Still. It'd been that kind of week.

"Sure."

"Attagirl," Zephyr said, lighting the joint. Weedsmoke mingled with the incense hanging in the air—an improvement, in Sabrina's opinion.

Zephyr puffed on the joint, then passed it to Sabrina. The harsh smoke made her cough—she had a brief flashback to the one time she'd smoked with Hal, who just said *coughing makes you higher* over and over again, laughing to himself about something that wasn't even a joke.

But it was good.

MAN, FUCK THIS HOUSE

She felt lighter, more relaxed. Maybe it was the drugs, maybe being out of the house, or just talking to another adult who wasn't her husband.

And didn't think she was crazy.

Either way.

"May I?" Zephyr said, motioning for the joint.

Sabrina blushed. "Sorry."

"You don't do this often, do you?"

"How'd you know?"

Zephyr waved dismissively. "How're you settling in?"

The question was enough of a blank envelope, the urge to confide in her new neighbor struck Sabrina, to let all the aggravations and uncertainties of the last few days out.

But she didn't.

"Fine," Sabrina said. "It's a beautiful house."

"Mm."

"Why didn't you want to come in the other day?" The question fell out of Sabrina's mouth before she even realized she'd said it—bold, for her.

Zephyr took another long puff on the joint. Exhaled, staring off into the distance.

Sabrina searched for something else to say, the last thing she wanted was to alienate the only non-Haskins she knew in the entire greater Jackson Hill area. "Sorry," she mumbled, moving to stand.

Zephyr put a hand on her thigh. "Sit."

Sabrina sat.

"Do you believe in the supernatural?" Zephyr asked.

Days before, Sabrina would've scoffed. She believed in God, vaguely, but that didn't count.

Ghosts, witches, demons—other than her kid? Pishposh.

Now?

"Yes," Sabrina said quietly.

"You've seen something, haven't you?"

Sabrina nodded.

"I thought so." Zephyr stubbed out the joint in an ashtray. "When I came over the other day, I—I didn't expect it. If that makes sense. Didn't expect anything. But when I crossed the threshold—well, I'm very sensitive. Ever had the shower turn cold on you?"

"Yes."

"That's what it's like. You're warm, hardly even thinking about how warm you are, and then—it's more than a chill. It's something else. But a shock, all right. That's what I felt. I should've been honest with you, but it surprised me so, I—I retreated. Ran off like a scared little dog."

"You've felt this before? Things like, like my house?"

"Oh yes. Like I said, I'm very sensitive. Ever since I was a little girl, I saw things, heard things, that other people couldn't. The world isn't what they tell you it is, I'm afraid." Zephyr smiled tightly, then looked away. "Most of the—I'll just say *things,* words like *ghost* are too loaded, full of false connotations— they're harmless. Don't even know you're there. But," she lowered her voice, as if she feared someone might be listening, "other things? They see us. And your house made me feel—"

"Seen."

"I'm not proud of leaving you in the lurch. But

there's something in your house, Sabrina. And I think you know this."

"Yes."

Zephyr drew a leg up underneath her. "Tell me everything."

Sabrina did. Every last detail, and many extraneous ones thanks to the weed. Zephyr listened patiently, nodding, sometimes asking a clarifying question.

When Sabrina finished, she realized she'd been gripping her coffee cup so hard the handle left an imprint in her palm.

"Incredible," Zephyr said. "I've never heard of such sustained activity."

"You've lived here a long time, haven't you?"

"Since 1983."

"So what happened? Was someone—" Sabrina hated to say it, "—*murdered* in my house?"

"Heavens no."

"And the neighborhood, it wasn't built on a cemetery?"

"This whole world's a cemetery," Zephyr said. "But no, nothing like that. It's a painfully ordinary neighborhood. Mostly bank-owned. Been years since anyone lived in your place. The man—I forget his name—was quite loud and messy, hardly kept the place up at all. But nothing VIOLENT ever happened there."

"Oh."

They finished their coffee, Zephyr chattering away about nothing at all—the town, her favorite restaurants, a yoga class Sabrina simply *had* to take. Eventually, Zephyr checked her watch and stood.

"Sorry, but I've got more chores I simply must get to. Come by again soon?"

"I will." Sabrina held up her coffee mug. "You want me to—"

"Just leave it on the table, will you?"

Sabrina headed for the door. Just as she opened it, Zephyr said, "Wait."

Sabrina turned, one hand on the knob.

"Something struck me. About your story. The things you've seen—a strange man carried a box down the basement steps. A bath appeared out of nowhere, morning coffee—"

"Yes?"

"None of it's . . . MALEVOLENT. Quite the opposite, actually. Have you ever thought that maybe you're just . . . lucky?"

"That's one way to think about it," Sabrina said slowly. "Thanks again." She left, trudging back to her own house. The one haunting her. Or helping her.

Thinking if this was luck, it was surely a strange sort.

Class was painful.

Even moreso than usual. Mr. Tuthill concluded their unit on Zack Snyder's *300* and moved on to recounting what Damien suspected was the plot of *Gladiator*—one of Hal's favorites—in embarrassingly animated fashion. Damien strongly believed pantomime had no place in the classroom, even if it was employed to reenact a sword fight that didn't occur two-thousand years before his birth.

MAN, FUCK THIS HOUSE

The entire performance was insufferable, and he stared at the clock counting the seconds and hoping for a good old-fashioned school shooting until the bell finally, mercifully rang.

Now to work.

His trip to Forever 31 complete, Damien had one more pressing piece of business to accomplish. Blood was an intrinsic part of his plan, but the fake stuff wouldn't cut it. Verisimilitude was the watchword, and one sniff of the Karo syrup-stuffed plastic pellets on the racks at the Halloween store told him they'd never do. He needed REAL blood, needed that iron tang to stoke Sabrina's atavistic impulses, send her spiraling headlong into a world of madness and terror.

Thankfully, you can find anything on the internet.

Damien skipped the school bus and boarded the city bus instead with a pocket full of cash divested from his sister's piggy bank.

After all, she owed him for bailing on the plan.

He leaned back in his seat, watching the city slide by. His phone buzzed—more mystery messages he could safely ignore—but then he noticed his data connection was far better than anywhere near the house on James Circle, and logged into *Fortnite* to pwn some noobs until the bus reached his destination.

Michaela watched her brother pass his bus, head down, never making eye contact with the driver. She was secreted in some bushes in front of the elementary school, leaning on her bike. Luckily, getting out of class was easy—she faked a stomachache, her medium-handsome teacher Mr. Delano asked if she had *lady problems,* and of course she swallowed her mortification and said yes, given that she was assuredly a lady with some very real problems.

Like finding out what her little brother was up to.

She'd long been a willing participant in Damien's schemes, although of late she'd found herself less a partner and more a fall guy—the infamous Columbus County Fair incident just one amongst several where she'd been caught holding her brother's bag. Suddenly, stricken of TV and video games and—God, Mom—TikTok privileges, Damien's antics didn't seem so funny anymore.

Definitely not now, with her mother seemingly teetering between sanity and its opposite.

A block away, Damien loitered around the city bus stop. She ducked into another stand of bushes to watch—her brother was maddeningly observant, but he seemed wrapped up in whatever he was doing.

A bus arrived, Damien got on. Michaela was faced with a difficult decision—board the bus and blow her cover, or lose him to the city.

Neither option seemed acceptable.

Through the bus window, she could see Damien bent down, focused on his phone. Probably *Fortnite.*

She pushed her bike out of the bushes and hopped on.

The bus pulled away from the curb, Michaela peddling furiously to keep up. A passing mom in an SUV gave her a weird look—kids her age didn't ride their bikes around Jackson Hill solving mysteries, apparently, like every other Netflix show—but Michaela ignored her, peddling furiously after the bus.

Luckily, the bus got caught at the next light. She caught up—careful to keep away from Damien's side—and leaned on her handlebars, panting heavily. It went like that for the next two miles, the bus pulling away over some distant hill, only to get snarled in traffic again. Once she feared she lost it altogether, came through an intersection thick with strip mall clusters, only to see it stopped a few dozen feet away.

Damien got off the bus, still engrossed in his phone. Seemingly without looking, he walked into the parking lot of a strip club called House of Jugs.

Gross!

She coasted down the sidewalk, veered behind a Cadillac. Set her bike down on the asphalt and poked her head around the taillights, trying to see what her brother was up to.

Damien was on his phone, talking animatedly. After a moment, a large man in overalls and a trucker hat came out of the strip club, swaying from side to side. He belched so loudly she could hear—and almost SMELL—him all the way across the parking lot.

Her brother handed the man a fistful of cash, who counted it, twice, nodding to himself, then ambled over to a rusty pickup with Truck Nutz hanging off the license plate. Two objects—canisters, vats, something—sat in the back.

Michaela inched around the Cadillac, slipped under an SUV. Commando-crawled closer to see what was going on.

"—but the best," the man was saying. "Drained 'em myself."

"Do I need to worry about diseases? Parasites?"

"Depends on what you plan on doing."

Damien giggled. "It's for a school project."

"Yeah, okay." The man lowered the gate.

Damien climbed up into the truck and popped the lid off one of the canisters. He recoiled, nearly fell out the tailgate. "Ugh!"

Michaela clamped a hand over her mouth to keep from yelling BE CAREFUL!

Damien steadied himself, then paused. His nose twitched, his gaze fanned the parking lot.

Michaela shrunk up under the SUV, pressing herself against a tire. Hoping he wouldn't see her, although she wasn't really sure why—if he knew she followed him, maybe he'd just abandon his idiotic plan.

As if.

The man said something unintelligible to Damien. He scanned the parking lot once more, then jumped down out of the truck bed. "Looks good. You can deliver?"

The man held out his hand.

Damien grumbled, then peeled off a few more bills. "Highway robbery."

"My cousin Terry works at the U-Haul. Guarantee my delivery fee's less'n what he'd charge to pretend like he saw a driver's license. Plus the booster seat rental."

"Very funny."

"Jokes're free, delivery ain't. We good?"

Michaela was still focused on the canisters in the

back of the truck. What in the world was Damien up to?

And where did he get all that money?

Damien tapped the side of the truck, slid a pair of child-size Ray-Bans over his eyes. "Pleasure doing business with you."

After coming back from Zephyr's, Sabrina drew a bath—on her own this time—and sank into the deliciously warm water. Fearless—with Hal home, she only worried about being judged. The water relaxed her, and the time alone, free from the state of hypervigilance she'd neurosed in for days, helped her get a little perspective.

She kept thinking about Zephyr's words—*nothing malevolent has happened.*

Had it?

Sabrina replayed every moment in the house from the day they'd arrived. Several disconcerting experiences, yes. But if she suppressed her fear of the unknown, looked at everything objectively, the actions of the house—and she felt a little crazy thinking that, as if Hal could peer into her mind and use it as ammunition later, when the men in white coats finally came to drag her out to a '58 Cadillac Sentinel—the actions of the house, like Zephyr said, were *hardly* hostile. The ghosts—again, crazy, silly—had done what, exactly? Made coffee? Drawn baths? Carried heavy boxes full of half-remembered belongings down to the basement? And then eaten their neighbor's disgusting SANDWICHES as a reward?

They hadn't threatened her, outwardly. Any threat was all in her head.

Except the dream she'd had, maybe. The man from the basement, barging into her bedroom.

But wasn't that in her head too? Hal saw nothing, heard nothing, except Sabrina freaking out. Maybe her mind had stitched her memories of the Experience together with her latent anxieties, whatever fears and trepidations were ping-ponging around her subconscious. What would Freud say? She'd taken Psych 110 before dropping out, she should know this stuff, although it always seemed a little snake-oily to her. Those psychiatrists, or psychologists, she could never remember who did what, they were all quacks anyway, weren't they? And in three weeks, Hal wanted her to go see one.

The house didn't.

The house, when she REALLY thought about it, didn't want anything from her.

Not like her daughter—rides, money, a minimum ten-foot distance at the mall.

Or her husband—dinners, lunches, and worst of all, impeccable mothering.

And her SON—what he actually wanted she couldn't articulate, SOMETHING bad. Her soul?

But the house, what did it want? Nothing, seemingly.

The house GAVE.

Maybe, she thought, dipping below the waterline, wetting her hair even though she didn't feel like shampooing it. *Maybe, maybe, maybe.*

Down there, below the bubbles, there seemed to be an awful lot of maybes. Far more than she'd ever had in the last fifteen years with Hal. Not since she was in college and her life was one big MAYBE.

Huh.

When she finally got out of the tub, there was a fluffy, clean towel folded up on the toilet seat.

Just waiting for her.

Damien didn't wake up, because he never really slept.

He'd stayed up late, and once the Haskins house was asleep, silently let himself out of his room. Finding the farmer had been a stroke of genius, albeit a very smelly one. The man had proved indispensable, providing Damien with everything he needed.

The delivery was scheduled for one a.m. Damien padded down the hall in his socks, not making a sound. He paused at Michaela's door. No light came from under the crack, and an ear to the wood yielded nothing but the familiar, rhythmic wheezes of sister-sleep.

Good.

Certain no one would interfere, Damien crept downstairs. He looked out the window—a dented truck idled in front of the empty house next door, lights off.

Damien listened once more for noises from upstairs—blessed silence—and reached for the doorknob.

BZZZZT.

His phone! Damien cursed silently to himself, pulling the infernal device from his pocket. He expected a simple text from the farmer—*I'm here, dude,* or some such banality—but no. The message was from that infuriating unknown number who'd bedeviled him ever since his arrival in Jackson Hill.

Don't.

Damien frowned. Who was this mystery texter, why were they so concerned with his business, and most importantly—

Were they WATCHING him?

Damien looked around, as if some hither-to unmet neighbor might be hiding in the shadows of the foyer. But no, he was alone. So who could—

Michaela.

The answer was obvious. She'd spoofed a fake number, in order to, to what, exactly? Unsettle and harass him? Derail his plans?

Damien smiled through his annoyance. He'd taught her well.

He powered off his phone, extended a middle finger at the ceiling, and then slipped outside to meet the farmer.

Amazingly, the man was as good as his word—Damien fretted all through dinner the farmer might simply run away with his money, but no, his country-fried honor bound him to the handshake deal he'd made with a ten-year-old. They unloaded the canisters of pig's blood and secreted them in the shed, the farmer surprisingly discreet, moving silently and keeping his redneck voice down.

Passing Michaela's door, he stopped again to listen for signs of life, but heard nothing.

In his room, he changed back into his SpongeBobs and slipped under the covers. His phone chirped.

Damien startled—it was OFF, he knew it was off.

Still, he reached for it. Yet another message waited for him.

You shouldn't do this. It's not nice.

Damien stifled the urge to toss the phone across the room. Instead he banged out a quick message—*meddle not in the affairs of Damiens, for you are stupid and your butt smells*—tapped send, and leaned back into his pillows, satisfied he'd totally owned her.

BZZT.

I'm serious.

No, Michaela, I'M serious. Don't stick your nose where it doesn't belong.

That seemed to shut her up. He turned the phone off again, just in case, and was about to fall asleep when it buzzed AGAIN.

I'm not Michaela.

And wasn't that exactly what Michaela would say? He shut the phone off—properly, this time, he hoped—and shoved it in his closet hamper. The issue resolved, he tried to go to sleep.

But couldn't.

Michaela Haskins slept soundly, and sent not a single text. From her own phone or any other.

THURSDAY

SABRINA AWOKE FIFTEEN minutes before the alarm.

Refreshed.

She stifled a yawn, looked over at Hal—blissfully asleep beside her, his hand tucked between cheek and pillow—and thought:

Wouldn't it be nice if Hal's lunch just made itself?

Wrapping her bathrobe around her—it smelled like detergent, even though she hadn't washed it since the move—she padded downstairs. The kids' backpacks, bookstuffed, waited next to the front door. Fresh coffee and a brown bag sat on the counter—that lunch she ordered. She opened the cabinet, checked the trash—empty, a brand-new liner in the can.

A girl could get used to this.

With little else to do, Sabrina poured coffee and settled on the couch, flipped on the TV, thinking she'd kill time with *Good Morning, America.*

Nothing but static.

Sabrina groaned, turned the TV off. Where was the cable guy, anyway? It'd been DAYS.

Wait.

Sabrina squeezed her eyes shut. Thought about watching TV. Pictured Robin Roberts, George Stephanopoulos, Michael Strahan, all of them, laughing and bantering their way through breaking news and pet tricks and interviews with Tom Hanks. Pictured herself, smiling along with her best friends.

Sad—that was sad, wasn't it?

No matter.

She imagined an Insta fitness guru she liked, this woman who wasn't annoyingly perfect—didn't airbrush her stretchmarks, at least. The guru was demonstrating a bosu ball routine, saying something about hip flexors. Michael Strahan said he wished *he* could be that flexible.

Everybody laughed.

Sabrina flipped on the TV.

"Good morning, America!" George Stephanopoulos said, flashing the camera a smile.

"Great to see you this morning," Robin Roberts added, giving Sabrina a thumbs up.

Sabrina returned it.

"We've got a very special guest today," George continued. "All the way from Jackson Hill—"

Michael Strahan popped up from behind the counter, grinning his gap-toothed smile. "That's my FAVORITE TOWN!"

Robin patted him on the head. "Okay, Michael. Here she is, our very special guest, Sabrina Haskins!"

Sabrina gasped. A woman walked out onstage, long silky hair shielding her face, wearing yoga pants and a navy tank-top. She waved at the audience—studio or otherwise—and plopped down on a couch next to the anchors, flipping back her hair.

It was HER.

Or a better version. This Sabrina didn't have chunky thighs, or a pooch, premature wrinkles, the subtle streaks of grey Hal insisted he couldn't see. She looked poised, confident.

AND she had Michelle Obama arms.

"So, Sabrina," George asked—and now he looked an awful look like Hal, actually— "we're delighted you could take some time out of your busy schedule to hang with us."

"So delighted!" Robin squealed.

"You're really setting the world on fire," Strahan said, popping out from behind the desk again. "With your, uh—" he squinted at an offstage teleprompter— "new blog!"

Was *that* it? Should she start a blog?

"Oh, it's more than just a blog, Michael," Screen-Sabrina said with a practiced studio-chuckle. "It's a virtual lifestyle destination. A comprehensive solution to help YOU—" she pointed a finger directly at the camera— "become the best YOU you can be. After all, I did!"

George nodded. "If anyone's an expert, it's you!"

"Tell me," Robin said, "how do I get Michelle Obama arms? Or maybe we should be calling them SABRINA HASKINS arms? Right?"

Sabrina winked. "That's why I'm here. Now, this might seem a little *feng shui*—" she wrapped scare quotes around her words— "but the first thing you've got to do is find a space that's conducive to self-actualization. Learn to trust it. Let it become a part of you. A good house anticipates your needs, after all. Knows you better than you know yourself."

Sabrina—the real Sabrina—nodded along. The conversation was at once very hard to follow AND made perfect sense. She'd learned so much from *GMA* over the years.

She really should keep listening now that SHE was on the show, no?

Sabrina made a mistake.

A BIG mistake.

Even when footsteps padded across the ceiling, indicating the others were up, she couldn't pry herself away from the TV. If anyone else came downstairs, what would they see?

Her, agog at an empty screen, probably.

GMA disappeared the second Hal poked his head into the living room and said, "Hun, have you seen my khakis?"

Sabrina dropped the remote. The screen was predictably filled with snow, static blared through the speakers.

She'd had the show up quite loud, apparently.

Sabrina grabbed the remote again, shut the screen off.

"What're you doing?" Hal said.

"Oh." She flailed for an answer until the box of movies by the TV saved her. "I was going to watch a... movie? I just—I don't suppose you have time to hook up the DVD before you go?"

"Can't you, I mean it's like two cords—" He caught himself. "Yeah, okay." Hal got on his hands and knees and started hooking up wires. Grumbling.

"Thanks, hun," Sabrina said. "I'll get your lunch. And coffee!"

In no way did Sabrina believe her deception had been remotely successful, and when he finally left he muttered something about trying to move her psychiatrist appointment up, but at least she was alone. Alone in the house.

Odd how things change, so quickly.

With nothing to do but wait for the delivery of her car, Sabrina went back into the living room, thinking she actually WOULD watch a movie. Why not? She sat a box of DVDs on the couch, flipped through the Haskins family film collection. Bizarrely eclectic— Sabrina preferred romantic comedies—*27 Dresses, What Happens in Vegas*, whereas Hal liked fart jokes and explosions. Michaela favored foreign films, although Sabrina suspected that was just her grasping at adulthood. Family movie nights usually turned into debates about what sort of movies were appropriate for a twelve-year-old.

For his part, Hal didn't so much take a side as unsubtly suggest they watch a Sandler flick instead.

Then there was Damien. After the three more vocal members finally settled on a *Mission: Impossible* since the series was frequently set in Europe and equally-frequently blew up its setting— they'd microwave popcorn and settle onto the couch, but Damien would sit cross-legged, facing his family, watching their reactions instead of the film. Sabrina found it profoundly unsettling.

Sabrina tossed a few of her usual choices onto the couch—*How to Lose a Guy in 10 Days* seemed appealing—but when she went to open the case, something stopped her.

She glanced at the TV.

Back at the movie.

Back at the TV.

GMA was probably wrapping up, but maybe the house would keep making the TV work for her. Nobody would be home for hours, anyway.

Sabrina raised the remote.

The screen flickered to life immediately—a commercial for cleaning supplies. Several bestial children, covered in filth with long ratty hair hanging in their faces, were in the process of destroying a kitchen that looked identical to her own. The children smashed glasses, smeared bloody fingerprints all over the cabinets. One hopped on the table until it broke, the legs rolling away. The other child—still unseen, all that dirty hair—picked up a table leg and started beating the other over the head.

"Hit me!" the recipient screamed, voice quavering with delight. "Hit me!"

The other child reared back, swung as hard as they could, the table leg arcing through the air—

The image froze, just before wood connected with jaw, the color leeching out of the scene in an instant.

"Keeping your kitchen clean isn't easy," a voice that sounded suspiciously like Sabrina's intoned over the still image. "Especially with a couple gremlins like THESE." The scene started again, Sabrina—hair bee-hived, blue cardigan over a flower-print house dress—entered, smiling like a Stephanopoulos.

"Good thing there's Nano-Clean from Sainz, the Bleach People™. With just two little squirts—" an orange bottle popped into Screen-Sabrina's hand. She poured bleach into two wineglasses on the counter. The feral children picked them up.

"I can make this whole mess—" Screen-Sabrina winked at the camera.

MAN, FUCK THIS HOUSE

"DISAPPEAR!" the children squealed, chugging their glasses like fratboys at dollar-beer night, hair flipping back to reveal Damien and Michaela's profiles.

"No!" the real Sabrina screamed. She hit the remote, nothing happened. She rushed the TV, searching for the plug. On-screen, the kids flopped to the ground, spasming, their spines bending back into question marks.

Recalling questions that ALWAYS went unspoken in the Haskins household.

Why'd you have me, for starters.

Sabrina froze, hand inches from the TV's power cord, an answer resounding in her mind, while the facsimiles of her children writhed and thrashed and puked up their guts on-screen.

Because I couldn't think of anything else to do.

She sank to her knees in front of the television, and stayed like that for a very long time.

At some point, Sabrina made her way back to the couch. Flipped channels. Found a court show, like *Judge Judy,* except *she* was the judge. And the plaintiff, the bailiff, the audience. Everybody was shouting incoherently.

She changed channels.

Some kind of cop show, Screen-Sabrina tracking down a murderer.

Click.

A soap opera—Hal had a very expensive suit and an eye-patch and might've been a doctor.

Click.

A game show—the set dressed like *The Price is Right,* a man with thick glasses reading from cue cards at a podium.

Sabrina squinted at the screen.

Her high school boyfriend, Darrell. No, Darren. Screen-Sabrina played all three contestants. Her children were the prizes—locked in a birdcage hovering over the stage.

All the contestants bet nothing, and everybody won.

KNOCK, KNOCK, KNOCK!

Sabrina reflexively hit the POWER button. The image onscreen disappeared.

KNOCK-KNOCK!

She stood, realizing she still wore her bathrobe. Decided she didn't care. Probably Zephyr, checking up on her.

She looked out the peephole. A swarthy man with a Chevy baseball cap stood on their stoop, inspecting his clipboard.

She frowned, opened the door a crack. "Hello?"

"Mrs. Haskins?" He jabbed a thumb over his shoulder. "Your van."

A flatbed sat in front of their house, her minivan on it.

Finally.

Sabrina listened to the man's spiel—the form required much initialing—then the flatbed groaned, dropping her minivan in the driveway. The man asked her if she had any questions.

She did. But none he could answer.

The flatbed drove off. She realized she still stood

in the doorway, keys in hand. Checked her watch—nearly one in the afternoon.

She was hungry.

Now that she had a car, she could go out to lunch. See what Jackson Hill had to offer, they were supposed to have nice restaurants. Maybe she could become a regular somewhere hip. A place where they put goat cheese on the salads.

"Huh," Sabrina muttered.

She dumped her keys in the dish next to the spare for the Camry and went back into the living room. The TV tray sat next to the couch, bearing a Caesar salad and a glass of red wine.

Sabrina sat down on the couch. Sipped wine—plum and tobacco notes—and inspected the salad.

Fresh-shaved parmesan, not goat cheese.

She shrugged and turned on the TV.

Damien got off the bus, excitement building. He'd had a rather good day at school—hot dogs for lunch, plus Mr. Tuthill seemed to be teaching *The Sword and the Stone* as actual history, the man's abject failure to even attempt to do his job was becoming endearing.

But now he was home, and far more exciting things awaited him.

Entering the cul-de-sac, Damien lowered his head to study the ground under his scuffed sneakers. Watched the world strictly through his peripherals. When he reached their front porch, Damien slipped off his shoes. Socked feet made less noise, and he preferred to move—and thus APPEAR—silently. A small part of him wished he could lumber about the house like his idiot father, and maybe someday he would. He'd never admit it to Michaela, but his lifelong prank HAD to have some sort of endgame. Why spend childhood pretending to be possessed if there wasn't a reveal at the end of it all?

Maybe this next one would be his last? He'd give Sabrina one good scare, and then come clean with the news he was just a normal—albeit super-intelligent— ten-year-old?

You must be joking.

Damien entered the foyer and paused, listening. The house was silent. Strange, because the family minivan—perhaps the most embarrassing conveyance known to man, a species that invented both the pogo stick and the unicycle—was finally here. Sabrina should be about, and yet he didn't hear any shuffling house slippers, clanging of pots and pans, or stifled sobs.

Damien sniffed the air, searching for that rank, motherly stink that had plagued him all his life— boiled radishes, although Michaela swore it was just in his head.

Now, though, the whole house reeked of bleach. Sabrina had been on a cleaning jag, evidently, despite the fact they'd only just moved in and the other Haskinses had yet to fully convert the place into their own personal pigpen. Damien nodded approvingly— perhaps she was turning over a new leaf.

A snore erupted from the living room—loud, rank, hoggish.

Damien peeked his head in. There she was, sprawled on the couch in her bathrobe. An empty wineglass sat on the coffee table—no coaster.

MAN, FUCK THIS HOUSE

He rolled his eyes—*of course* she'd become a cliché. Or even more of one, college dropout to stay-at-home mother was a well-trod path. A blood test would probably reveal the presence of all sorts of pharmaceuticals. He gave the room a cursory glance, noting the static pouring from the television, the DVD cases strewn on the floor at the foot of the couch, the remote still clutched in her hand.

Shook his head at the sad, sad scene.

A flicker of something—empathy, maybe—flared in the back of his mind, but he dismissed it. If anything, the tableau in front of him made him even more sure of the course he'd chosen.

Sabrina was asking for it.

He stood over her for ten minutes, slack-jawed, hoping she'd wake up and scream at the sight, but no. Annoyed, he stalked upstairs, reminding himself of the afternoon's silver lining.

She had a car, finally. The second he had the house to himself, he could enact his plan.

Yet another message from Michaela's alt—*leave her alone.*

He sent her back a picture of Johnson's Baby Shampoo—*No More Tears*—and went about his business.

Sabrina Haskins woke up feeling like her phone had been ringing for a VERY long time. She blinked, looked down at her phone, just as it stopped buzzing.

Eleven missed calls.

All from the same unfamiliar number. No messages.

Sabrina was about to call the number back when her phone rang again. Same number.

"Hello?"

"Mrs. Haskins?" The voice was male, deep, flat. Business-like.

She was pretty sure they were paid up on all their bills.

"This is she," Sabrina replied, rising off the couch. Her legs swayed, unsteady from an afternoon's disuse. She planted a hand on the couch's arm.

"Ah, hello." A muffled cough echoed from the other end. "We haven't met. Bill Ramstead. Hal's boss?"

"Oh, hi." Sabrina poked her head into the kitchen to check the microwave clock. *4:30.* "What can I do for you?"

"Sorry to call you like this," Ramstead said, "but your husband is in the hospital."

"Hal?" As if she had another.

"Started getting stomach pains after lunch. We thought it was just indigestion, but about an hour later Reina found him passed out on the floor in his office. Paramedics said they'd have someone call you from the hospital. They didn't, huh?"

"No?"

"That's bureaucracy for you. Well, glad I called then. Hal's tough, I'm sure he'll pull through. But, uh, you might want to get over there, see what's going on. Jackson Hill Presbyterian. You know it?"

"We're new."

"'Course you are. I can send Reina to get you."

Sabrina looked out the window. "My car finally came."

MAN, FUCK THIS HOUSE

"How about that. You change your mind, give me a call, okay?" Ramstead clicked off.

Sabrina stood there, phone to her ear, wondering if the conversation had actually happened, or if it was like the TV—real-ish, an illusion bordering on *de*lusion. Maybe it was the house, pretending to be Hal's boss, although why it would do such a thing—

One way to find out.

She found the hospital, a sprawling, ultramodern glass complex with numerous outbuildings—the Crain Cardiology Institute, Hutchinson Center for Obstetrics and Gynecology. Sliding into a visitor space, she kept thinking about the Camry back at Hal's office. Likely would sit there until Hal recuperated because who'd help Sabrina bring it home? Reina, whoever that was? Zephyr probably rode a bicycle—maybe a broomstick—and Michaela was YEARS away from even asking for her learner's permit.

Locking the car, it occurred to Sabrina she'd decided this was very serious, even though for all she knew Hal might just need an IV and some Zofran.

Food poisoning, right?

Strange, she was always so careful, washed her hands and wiped the counter after handling raw chicken, eggs—

Except SHE hadn't made Hal's lunch, had she?

"'Scuse me, ma'am," an orderly muttered, nearly knocking her over with a cart loaded down with hospital supplies. Sabrina had wandered right into reception without even realizing it. She approached the front desk, gave her name. They directed her to a very uncomfortable plastic chair, where she waited for an interminable amount of time before someone told her to go up to the third floor. Sabrina wandered until she found a nurses' station, got further directions, and finally ended up in Hal's room.

Of course he was asleep.

She didn't want to wake him, so she sat down in another uncomfortable chair until a nurse came in to check Hal's vitals. The woman grunted at Sabrina's questions, scribbled on a clipboard, and said someone would be along soon.

Sabrina watched Hal sleep—peaceful, very peaceful, aside from the flushed skin and sweat beading his brow—and wondered if he was dreaming.

Footsteps clicked down the hall. A woman entered—pantsuit, hair pulled back in a loose ponytail. She looked nothing like a doctor, everything like a cop.

"Mrs. Haskins?"

Everyone was calling her that now. Sabrina was so used to *mom* and *hun* and other familiar diminutives, even 'Brina, Hal's idiot shorthand because three syllables were one too many for him. *Mrs. Haskins* felt strange, foreign, even though she'd been exactly that for a third of her life.

"Sabrina," Sabrina said, standing.

The woman motioned for her to remain seated. Sabrina noticed she didn't carry a purse.

"Detective Sherman," the woman said, extending a hand—short, well-manicured nails, a simple gloss.

Sabrina took her hand without thinking. "I'm waiting for the doctor."

MAN, FUCK THIS HOUSE

"Just spoke with her. A Dr. Gaddipati. She seems very good."

Sabrina nodded. "That's, uh, what you want, I guess."

"Mm." Sherman gestured at the doorway. "Mind if we talk in the other room? It'll just take a moment."

"Sure?"

Sherman moved away from the door, waited for Sabrina to get up, then drew alongside her. She guided Sabrina to a small break room, where they sat at a round table covered in crumbs. The detective pulled a small spiral-bound notebook from her pocket. "Mind if I take a few notes?"

"No?"

"Great." She drew one leg over the other. "What've they told you so far?"

"Nothing, I haven't talked to anyone." Sabrina scratched at the dirt trapped under a nail. "You're a police detective?"

"Correct."

"What's—what's a *police detective* doing here?"

"Just detective's okay." Sherman's nostrils twitched. "Have you been drinking, Mrs. Haskins?"

"No?"

Sherman scribbled something on her notepad. "You're new here, right?"

"As of last Saturday."

"Welcome." Sherman looked up from her notes, gave a passably genuine smile. "Getting settled?"

Sabrina shrugged.

"Moving's a real nightmare," Sherman said. "I'm from Boulder, originally. But it's a great community, really is. Have you been to R.J. Fluffernutter's?"

"No?"

"What passes for culture, here. Video games, ski-ball, stuff like that. Your kids will love it. You have kids, right?"

"Michaela. And Damien."

Sherman scribbled. "That's great. I love kids. Always thought I'd have a couple of my own by now."

"I'm sure with the job, it's—it's tough. Meeting someone."

"You can say that again. Cops date cops, and if you've seen the department—" Sherman arched an eyebrow, *gosh, can you believe what I'm stuck with?*

"Anyway. Think you met one of my colleagues a few days ago, actually. Officer Stephens?"

Sabrina could barely picture the man, but she nodded anyway.

"Got an update for you," Sherman said. "We'll get to that in a second. How're things with you and Hal?"

"Good?"

"No fights? Moving can be a real strain."

Sabrina shook her head, confused as to where this was going.

"That's good. Look, the reason I'm here, Sabrina— I can call you Sabrina, yes?"

"Yes?"

"Reason why I'm here, the doctors ran some preliminary tests and it looks like Hal might have ingested something. Pretty routine, covering all the bases. He's going to be okay, by the way."

"He is?"

Sherman fixed her with a strange look. "People usually ask that."

"Ask what?"

MAN, FUCK THIS HOUSE

"If they'll be okay. Their loved ones. Have you and Hal had any arguments lately?"

"No!" But they had, hadn't they? Sabrina's chest tightened—what if they knew about the psychiatrist? The outburst at dinner? But what did this have to DO with anything?

"Mm," Sherman muttered, writing. Writing writing writing.

She asked more oddly specific questions, whether Sabrina made Hal's lunch or not—and how could she answer THAT, without lying or sounding like a complete loon?

Clearly, she said *yes*.

After asking the same five questions seemingly a few dozen times, Sherman set her pad aside and fixed Sabrina with a serious look. "I need to ask this, specifically. And you need to be honest with me, Sabrina. Can you do that? Be honest?"

Sabrina nodded.

"Has Hal ever hit you?"

Sabrina sucked in a quick breath, like she'd been punched. "Of course not."

The detective's eyes never strayed from Sabrina's. "He's in the other room, he can't hear you. Anything you want to tell me—"

"Hal's never hit me." The thought had never even crossed Sabrina's mind. A couple of her other boyfriends, the guys who came wrapped in leather jackets, pulling cocaine-crusted dollar bills out of their chain wallets to buy her an extraordinarily late dinner at Waffle House—those boyfriends, they hadn't hit her either, but with one or two sometimes she'd said something, and all of a sudden the air stilled—highly pressurized, like right before a storm when you can smell the rain on the wind—and that single moment stretched out so long she thought if she blinked she'd find herself on her back, in a hospital bed.

Not like with Hal. Sure, they fought, said things they shouldn't, just like anyone did.

But he'd never raised a fist to her in anger, nor she to him, and Sabrina knew neither of them ever could.

The detective didn't.

"I'd tell you," Sabrina said. "I promise."

Sherman reached in her suit jacket, handed Sabrina a card. "My personal cell's on there."

Sabrina slid the card into her purse. "You said you had some news? About the—" she struggled to find the right words, "—prowler?"

"Right. One second." The detective pulled out her phone, scanned what Sabrina presumed to be an email. "Question for you, first. The box Officer Stephens dusted for fingerprints? That was left by the previous owners?"

"No, it was ours. Why?"

"Mm." Sherman tapped a nail on her phone screen. "Ordinarily this stuff takes FOREVER—" she rolled her eyes, *the slowly-turning wheels of justice, amirite?* "—but we actually had the perp's fingerprints in the system. Longtime friend of ours."

"He is?"

"Have you ever met a Dirk Perryman?"

"No, I don't think so."

"See, that's why I asked if the box came with the house. Mr. Perryman is a former resident."

MAN, FUCK THIS HOUSE

Sabrina blinked. "He is? Did he—" she swallowed, her mouth awfully dry, "—DIE in the house?"

"Huh?" Detective Sherman gave her a weird look. "Perryman's not dead. In fact, he's in prison."

"What?"

"Vehicular manslaughter. Really nasty, but before my time. Prior to that, he was well acquainted with Jackson Hill PD. Ran a bit of a party house. Booze, drugs. A real nuisance."

The gears in Sabrina's mind turned. "You're SURE he's in prison?"

"Checked myself. Not going anywhere, either. He's got a bit of an attitude problem."

"Oh." Nothing about it made sense. How had a convict gotten his fingerprints on THEIR box? Even if he used to live there?

"Do you—do you have a picture of him?"

Sherman shrugged, pushed her phone into Sabrina's hands. "Knock yourself out."

Sabrina stared down at the phone screen. A black and white mugshot stared back at her—a large man, piggish eyes, vaguely drunk expression.

The same man Sabrina had seen in her basement, without question.

The room swirled around her. "I don't feel so good."

"Well," Sherman said, standing. "This is the place for it."

Jackpot.

Damien was alone, finally. No Sabrina, no

Michaela, no Hal—not that his father would have noticed anything amiss, anyway.

Now he could begin.

Damien stepped out into the backyard. The shed door was half-open—dumb move, he must've left it like that the evening before, when the farmer delivered his supplies. Thankfully Michaela hadn't nosed around.

Unless SHE left the door open.

Damien ran to the shed, stuck his head inside. Something landed in his hair, he yelped, brushed it out. Couldn't see what—a dark shape skittered under the lawnmower. He thought about yanking the rip cord, pureeing the disgusting little creepy crawly, but he didn't have time.

Donning a pair of work gloves—shaking them out first, naturally—Damien grabbed the first canister of blood, hauled it bow-legged into the house. He set the vessel in the mudroom, then went back and got the other. Hauling them upstairs proved more of a chore, but with the proper motivation and plenty of naughty words, Damien moved everything into its proper place.

Rigging the device above Sabrina's bedroom doorway was easy by comparison. He'd designed the contraption with his usual brilliance, had no doubt it would work.

With the tripwire set, he stole one of Michaela's old baby dolls—the most realistic one he could find—and slathered it in blood. Just a little something to wave around.

Then he went downstairs to enact Phase 3. A little symbology would go a long way. He took a knife from the kitchen, shoved the coffee table out of the way, and started carving a pentagram in the floor.

His phone kept going off—more texts, certainly—but he paid it no mind. Michaela could try to stop him, but there was nothing she could—

"What are you doing?" his sister shrieked, standing in the doorway.

Damien ignored her, kept etching.

So intent on his task he never noticed a hundred pounds of angry sister-weight barreling down on him.

Sabrina drove home from the hospital, head spinning.

The last few hours had really done a number on her. Hal woke up—confused, but seemingly out of the woods. The doctors were running some additional tests and planned to continue monitoring him for at least another day. They had questions, too, asking after Hal's allergies, diet, where she bought groceries. The detective, Sherman, had hovered, at times obsequious, asking Sabrina if she wanted coffee, at other times silent, staring.

Judging.

Sabrina didn't care for her at all, or the way she thought she heard a nurse say *poison*.

She cared even less for the information the detective shared. Who was this Dirk Perryman, anyway? If he'd died in the house, that would make A LITTLE sense—spooky sense, Halloween sense. This didn't. How had a living man, sitting in a correctional facility, managed to apply HIS fingerprints to a Haskins family moving box?

How had Sabrina SEEN him?

Her phone rumbled on the seat next to her. *Michaela.* Sabrina realized she'd not told either of her children what had happened to their father, or where she was, and wondered if she was the worst wife and mother on the planet.

She didn't have her AirPods, so she tucked the phone between her chin and shoulder. "Hello?"

"Mom? Where are you?"

"On the way home." Should she say something now? Or what, sit Michaela down? God knew Damien wouldn't so much as blink at the news his father had been hospitalized.

"Ookay. What're we doing for dinner?"

Sabrina hadn't even thought of that. "Order pizza," she said. "Put it on the card in the drawer." *The one you've been using to buy movies on iTunes,* Sabrina almost added.

"Pizza AGAIN?" Michaela said.

The phone slipped, Sabrina pushed her jaw into her shoulder to keep it in place. "I'm almost home, just—"

"Oh, I guess Damien ordered pizza," Michaela said.

"What?"

Sabrina could hear her daughter's footsteps over the phone, clomping through the house like a wildebeest. "There's a pizza on the counter. From—" Sabrina could almost picture her bent over the pizza box, squinting, Michaela hated her glasses and their old optometrist said she wasn't ready for contacts yet— "some place called Morio's?"

"Mario's?"

"No, Morio's. With an *O.*"

"Throw it away."

"What?"

A cop pulled out from a side street up ahead. Sabrina flipped on the speakerphone, keeping it level with the dash so it wouldn't look like she was merrily flaunting the state's hands-free law. "I said throw it away."

"But Damien—"

"Your brother didn't order it!" Not that Damien would order pizza, anyway—too helpful. "I'll explain when I get home. Just don't eat anything. In fact, take your brother and—"

The cop suddenly pulled over to the side of the road—no lights—and Sabrina dropped the phone in her lap so he wouldn't see.

"Mom?" Michaela called, voice muffled by Sabrina's lap. "Mom?"

"Hold on," Sabrina shouted. She passed the cop, kept her eyes locked on the rearview, petrified he'd flip his flashers on.

The cop stayed put. Sabrina fished the phone out of her lap. "I'll be home in five minutes." She had no idea how far away she was. "Don't do anything until then, okay?"

"Ugh, fine. This is so dumb," Michaela said.

"See you soon," Sabrina said, thumb moving to end the call.

"Mom?"

"What?"

Sabrina drove past a street she was 90% sure was the one she wanted. She needed to get off the phone, give up on understanding the Byzantine layout of her new town, and Google their darn address.

"I don't want to..." Michaela said, voice hazy and insubstantial. "Mom—" stronger now, firmer—"Damien's planning something."

This was the last thing she needed right now. "What do you mean?"

"He's—he's obsessed with messing with you, okay?"

"Messing with me?"

"That's what he's all about, making you—crazy. And he's got this new idea, I don't know all the details, but he's—I want you to know so you're not scared, because it's scaring me, and—"

Sabrina understood precisely nothing of what her daughter was saying. Damien, planning something? He was malicious, certainly, but developmentally stunted.

It sounded ridiculous.

"I'll be home soon," Sabrina said, ending the call. She thumbed over to the maps app and tried to type in their address while keeping her eyes on the road.

Sabrina pulled into the driveway a little after six. A pang struck her, that same worry about Hal's car, what they'd do with it. She got out and paused, a strange, whirring sound drawing her attention.

Plus the scent in the air—freshly cut grass.

The sound grew louder, coming from the backyard, and then HE came around the side of the house.

Dirk Perryman.

The man who was supposedly in prison—and not

a very nice person at all, to hear Detective Sherman tell it.

He pushed a rusty red-and-white mower, the canvas bag fat with grass clippings. Sweat drenched his brow, stained his t-shirt. He stopped next to the downspout, stepped away from the mower, and wiped his forehead with an old bandana.

"Hey!" Sabrina yelled, then reflexively clamped a hand over her mouth.

Perryman startled, dropped the sweaty bandana on the ground.

Then saw her.

And smiled.

"Oh, you scared me," he said, voice so deep *scared* sounded more like *scarred*.

Sabrina gaped. "I scared YOU?"

"Gotta go!" Perryman shouted. He dropped to his hands and knees, baby-crawled to the downspout—a hysterically tiny aperture—and pushed his head inside, skull squishing, God help her, SQUISHING like Play-Doh to fit. His massive paws scrabbling at the dirt for leverage, pushing his bulk further into the piping inch by inch, skin stretching like taffy. The downspout bulged and shook, all the way to the gutters, like a boa swallowing a particularly tenacious mouse.

"What the what," she mumbled.

"Mom!" Michaela called.

Sabrina glanced over at the front porch. Her daughter stood there, hands on hips, an odd look on her face.

"Who are you talking to?" Michaela asked.

Sabrina waved her away, stumbled towards the

door. She couldn't begin to process what she'd seen, to slot it into her mental rolodex of incredibly messed-up phenomena witnessed over the last six days. She needed to get inside, dispose of the mystery pizza, and then—

What?

Leave? Stay? Burn 4596 James Circle to the ground and salt the earth?

She couldn't even make up her mind about the house. One second it was terrifying, the next helpful. She'd been sleeping like crap, nothing seemed to make sense. Had the house ACTUALLY done something to Hal? Was it trying to do something similar to the rest of her family?

How could she know, and what should she do about it?

If anything.

Sabrina stopped just before the door.

Michaela looked at her strangely. "Mom?"

"Come look at this," Sabrina said, grabbing her daughter's wrist. Michaela tried to shy away, but Sabrina held tight, pulled her down the front steps.

"Ow," Michaela said. "I can walk."

"Sorry." Sabrina released her grip—red marks remained, fingerprints standing in stark relief against her daughter's skin—

Evidence

—but then they faded.

Michaela rubbed her wrist, glaring at Sabrina. "What are you showing me?"

"Over here," Sabrina said, rounding the house—the downspout looked utterly normal and obviously incapable of swallowing a man whole—and pointed to the abandoned lawnmower, sitting in an unfinished strip of grass.

"So?" Michaela crossed her arms. "That's Damien's job."

Cutting the lawn was one of the few tasks allotted to the youngest Haskins sibling. They didn't trust him with it—that would be ridiculous, giving a kid like that unfettered access to a pair of whirring blades and a whole gallon of gas—so he did his duty under heavy supervision from Hal.

Who for his part mostly sipped beers and listened to sports talk radio on his phone, but thus far no one had lost a finger.

"Damien wasn't doing it," Sabrina said. "When I came home—this man used to live here. The police told me. He's in prison, so he SHOULDN'T be here, but he is, I saw him cutting the grass and then—" Sabrina kicked the spout, gently.

"I don't understand, what—"

Sabrina threw her head back and screamed— actually SCREAMED—at the sky, a burst of anger and frustration that sent the crows perched on the neighbor's tree running for cover. The cry echoed in the late afternoon air. Her head sank into her chest, tears filled her eyes. She leaned against the house, forehead pressed against the cool aluminum siding. Her chest hitched, she thought she might fall to pieces.

She stood there, for a very long time, worried she was losing her mind.

Terrified she already had, and would never, ever know.

Michaela called Mom's name, tugged her sleeve, poked her. Nothing. Mom—increasingly unhinged these last few days, even to a twelve-year-old's eye— had gone catatonic, apparently driven mad by—

The lawn?

Almost funny—Damien had been plotting and scheming for so long, coming up with ever-more-elaborate ways to manipulate their mother, when all he needed to do was neglect his chores? Figured— Michaela took real pride in hers, but her parents rarely noticed. Just because Damien acted so weird, HE got all the attention—

Damien wasn't cutting the grass.

After catching him carving his pentagram, Michaela dragged him upstairs by his ear. He'd pleaded with and threatened her, but she wouldn't budge, and she was still a few inches bigger than him. No matter what, she resolved to tell their parents his secret and put an end to his nonsense once and for all.

Then Mom called, Michaela tried to tell her— dodging stink faces from Damien the whole time—but Mom wouldn't listen, Dad was nowhere to be found, and SOMETHING was going on but as per usual nobody told Michaela anything, and then the little— she grit her teeth, trying to come up with the right word to describe her brother—the little SO-AND-SO slipped away.

To mow the yard?

Maybe Damien started his chores before she'd gotten home—even though he wasn't supposed to use the mower without Dad—then taken his pentagram-carving break.

Whatever, she needed to figure out what to do about Mom.

Michaela went inside, got her phone from the living room. She dialed Dad's cell. No answer—should she call 911? That was only for emergencies, and Mom didn't seem HURT, she wasn't bleeding. Michaela didn't want to get in trouble.

"Damien!" she finally called. "Damien!"

No answer.

Of course he was no help, this was his sick little dream come to life. Back when it was all a game, and especially when Michaela was royally P.O.'ed at her parents, such an outcome seemed funny, because it was so clearly a fantasy. Michaela always thought Damien, for all his precocious genius, would only succeed in making Mom believe he shouldn't be allowed to use the adult scissors.

But now?

Mom flipping out over the grass, screaming nonsense at the sky, breaking down in tears?

CRAZY wasn't some far-off country, some esoteric destination to which they'd never arrive, paired with a journey steeped in delight, whimsy, and secretive sibling bonding as the Haskins kids Lemony-Snicketed their way out of childhood.

CRAZY was here. And it scared her.

"Damien?" she tried one more time, louder.

The house groaned in response.

Michaela headed out the door. Her mother still leaned against the side of the house, face in hands, still as the aluminum siding. Unresponsive.

Mom . . .

Michaela scrolled through her contacts, all hundreds of miles away. None of them could help her. Who—

The neighbor!

Her and Mom were friendly, right?

Loath as she was to admit it, she very badly needed an adult.

Damien crept around the side of the house, moving in a crouch like *Fortnite*—completely silent. Except this time, he wasn't gripping a shotgun in an avatar's animated hands.

This time, he had something far better.

As soon as Michaela got distracted by the phone call, he'd slipped past her. Hidden in the hall closet, behind the laundry basket, pouting. He'd put so much effort into this, and now his stupid sister was going to ruin everything.

Until the screaming started.

Damien knocked over the laundry basket, spilling soiled socks and underwear into the hallway. He peeked out his parents' window. Down in the yard, Michaela fussed over a seemingly frozen Sabrina, who seemed to be having some kind of fit, then ran back in the house. She called his name, but he didn't answer. Then she left again. He moved to his own window, watched her hurry across the street.

Very strange.

Damien crept downstairs and out the back to see what the fuss was all about. Maybe they'd found a dead cat or something. Why that would send Michaela running for the neighbor's, he couldn't fathom, but nothing about the odd tableau he'd witnessed made much sense.

Rounding the side of the house, the first thing he noticed was the lawnmower, the partially-cut strip of grass. Who'd been doing yardwork? Michaela? He hated it, but it was HIS job to hate, not hers. Instinctively, he laid the back of his free hand against the motor.

Still warm.

Strange.

But stranger still was the sight presented when he rounded the corner—Sabrina burrowing her face into the aluminum siding, tears streaming down makeup-smeared cheeks, shoulders hitching. Lank hair plastered to her forehead, a ghoulish pallor in her skin.

Damien froze, unsure what he'd walked in on, and some primal emotion cut through years of bored disdain. Reflexively, without a care for the long, long chess game he'd played, a single word popped out of his lips.

"Momma?"

Sabrina gulped, her head turned inexorably slowly in his direction, her eyes met his, took in her youngest child, or the thing he'd made himself into for her detriment.

Her eyes went wide, filled with fear and knowing.

Again.

Once more.

She screamed.

Monster.

She'd known all along, since Dr. Sapirstein told her Damien consumed his womb-mate, stolen any chance she'd ever have to know and love her THIRD child, and now here IT was, right in front of her, proof positive she'd been right, right, right.

The Damien she'd known was gone, replaced by—there was no other word for it, a DEMON. His skin was blood-red, twisted horns grew from his forehead, yellow cats'-eyes blazed in the dark recesses of his skull. He cradled a bloody fetus under his arm like a normal boy might a football helmet—his dead sibling, perhaps?

And worst of all, he called her *Momma*—his voice a mocking parody of a child's love, like the gravelly pit-birthed blasphemies of the demon inside Regan, the scorn-drenched timbre a refutation of the word itself, and all the weight that came with it.

Momma, Mom, Ma, Mother, Madre, Mère, Mutter, Mor, Matka.

Any diminutive of *Mother*, in any language, from THAT mouth?

A lie, its only meaning malice.

She fled wailing, the word—*Momma*—flung at her back, again and again, the demon-thing's voice ratcheting between plaintive and hysterical but every word adrip with profound mockery.

Reaching the house, Sabrina fell up the front steps, banging her knees, biting her tongue. She flung herself at the door. It opened—for her—and she fell into the house.

MAN, FUCK THIS HOUSE

The door slammed shut.

Sabrina fumbled with the deadbolt until it slammed home. Looked around, breathing heavily. Her gaze settled on the living room—disturbed, and disturbing, a partially-finished pentagram carved into the floor, black candles arranged around it.

The air reeked of blood.

She felt sick. That was what Michaela tried to tell her? Damien had—what, exactly? Summoned up his true self from Hell, which apparently existed in an entirely literal sense?

Never mind the pentagram lay unfinished, a rough scratching in their beautiful hardwood floors. She had no clue how those things worked.

All she knew was this: Hell was here. In her home.

And since the moment a bad bolt of sperm poisoned a wicked egg, it always had been.

Damien was knocking on the front door—POUNDING—and yelling muffled things in his ancient, deceiver's voice. Sabrina ran to the back door, locked that too.

The locks couldn't hold him for long, could they? Panting, desperate, her eyes alighted on the knife rack.

But she quickly looked away. Pressed her hands together in prayer—awkward, unfamiliar—and offered up half-remembered words of devotion to a God who, logically, should actually be listening, all things considered.

In response, the TV in the living room turned on, blaring a commercial for some new kind of laundry detergent.

So loud she couldn't hear the bathtub upstairs, starting to run.

Damien ran after his mother—*Momma*—but her legs were far longer, propelled by terror. This was the result he expected, the result he desperately desired, Sabrina FLEEING from him, stricken with fear, and yet he knew, viscerally and intellectually, that he hadn't caused any of this.

Made it worse, maybe.

She fell on the porch, threw herself through the doorway, slammed the door in his face.

Damien stood on the front porch, panting. Reached for the doorknob—locked.

He felt ridiculous. Beyond ridiculous. Caked with dime store demon makeup, chasing a grown woman, and a mentally ill one at that.

What had he become?

Damien reached up, grabbed a horn, ripped it away, leaving a tacky residue of spirit gum on his brow. He tossed it in the bushes. Reached for the other one—

And froze when the porch groaned under a weight three times his own.

Damien, half-horned, whirled around. A man stood on the steps—large, dirty, wearing a once-white t-shirt, belly straining the fabric. He had a very square head, short hair.

A wide grin strained his face.

"You're Damien, right?"

Damien's head whipped from one neighboring house to the other, to the curb, trying to figure out if the man was simply a neighbor he'd not met, or a landscaper, or—

MAN, FUCK THIS HOUSE

Or.

"How do you know my name?" Damien asked.

"I've been helping out your mother," the man said, cocking his chin at the house. "She needs a LOT of help."

Damien couldn't exactly disagree. But still. "Who ARE you?"

The man chuckled, gazing down at the porch steps. "I'm me. And you're you. And Damien? I'm sorry to say this, but—" he fixed Damien with a very serious stare, the kind of look parents and teachers gave him when he'd crossed a line, "—you've made things VERY difficult for your mother.

"And we simply can't have that."

The man lunged.

Damien jumped back, the doorknob slammed into his lower back, and then the man had him, wrapped up in a bearhug, pressing Damien's face into his chest, and he couldn't SEE anything, but he could smell—a thick, overwhelming, cloying, horribly FAMILIAR miasma of scents. Not male musk and grass clippings, as his appearance might suggest, but wood, mothballs, dust, bleach, baking cookies.

Just like their house.

Michaela raised a fist to pound on the door, then froze, mid-air—she didn't want to look *crazy*—and rang the doorbell instead.

Shot a look over her shoulder—her mother was fixated on something around the side of the house. Disturbing, but at least she hadn't gone anywhere.

No one came to the door. Michaela rang the doorbell again, shuffling from one foot to the other like she had to pee. She tried the bell one last time, about to give up and call 911—they wouldn't lock up a twelve-year-old if she really WAS worried, right?— when muffled footsteps resounded from inside the house. Michaela exhaled a sigh of relief.

The door opened. An aged woman stood there— older than Mom—wearing what looked like a carpet. She raised an eyebrow at the tween on her doorstep.

"Help you?"

"I'm Michaela Haskins, from across the street?" She turned to point at their new house, and if she'd been a hair faster she might've seen the man with Dirk Perryman's fingerprints disappearing into the side yard, her little brother in a headlock.

The woman—Zephyr, her name was—mock-curtsied. "I finally get to meet the OTHER lady of the house. Selamat siang, young miss. As they say."

Michaela didn't know anyone who said that. "My mom? She's acting—"

"Funny? Peculiar? Passing strange? Can't say I'm surprised. That house..." The woman trailed off, staring into the distance.

"I need your help," Michaela said. "I don't know what to—"

Zephyr held up a hand. "Say no more! Come in while I get a few things. I'm going to do what I should have done a long, long time ago."

Michaela blinked. "What's that?"

Zephyr clenched a fist. "I'm going to exorcise the pants off that horrible, horrible house.

"With prejudice."

MAN, FUCK THIS HOUSE

Sabrina was on *Sixty Minutes*. And *Dateline, 20/20, 60/40, Real Sports with Bryant Gumbel, Fake Sports with Byron Grimble, Clarissa Explains It All,* and *Hannity,* which would have impressed her noddingly-conservative husband.

Were he not languishing in a hospital bed.

Every time Sabrina flipped the channel, there SHE was, laughing with the anchors, chatting, perfectly-coiffed and looking FAR more beautiful than all the Insta-Mommies combined. She finally settled on a show called *Everywhere Tonight.*

"Tell me, Sabrina," an incredibly handsome, chin-dimpled specimen asked—stars in HIS eyes, agog at her glory. "How do you do it? You've got your fitness empire, pillowcase and duvet line, the *New Peanuts* comic strip?"

Screen-Sabrina laughed—an aggressive, mirthless LadyBoss laugh that would make her inevitably-nerdy assistant pee her pants in terror—and waved dismissively. "I can't take ALL the credit, DanKeith. I've got a little help."

The camera panned over to the side of the stage, where Dirk Perryman—or the thing passing as him—entered stage left, still wearing his filthy, stained t-shirt and ripped jeans, but the crowd went wild anyway. Screen-Perryman clasped his hands high over his head and waggled them, mugging for the audience.

"So glad you could join us," DanKeith said. "When we come back, [BLEEP] and I will talk about some

MAJOR CHANGES coming to the Haskins household.

Screen-Sabrina winked at the camera. "About time we shook things up around here!"

"Just like a baby!" Screen-Perryman added, pantomiming a shaken infant. He tossed the imaginary baby to DanKeith, who planted it feet-first in an equally-invisible blender and made pitch-perfect whirring sounds.

The anchor wiped imaginary baby-guts off his forehead with the sleeve of his suit jacket, then smiled into the camera. "Be right back!"

Damien kicked, scratched, clawed, but the big man who smelled like their house wouldn't let him go. "Get off me!" he yowled.

The man clamped a meaty paw over his mouth.

Not that there was anyone to care—his mother would've welcomed his abduction at any point during the last decade, but especially now. Michaela'd gone from co-conspirator and confidant to arch-enemy in the space of a day. Maybe this was her play, hiring some sicko off the dark web to do away with him, so he wouldn't torment her precious mother. What had Sabrina ever done for Michaela, anyway?

Nothing.

Served him right for ever letting a lesser light in on his plans in the first place.

The man drug him around the side of the house, past the mower—Damien had visions of his captor yanking the rip cord, shoving his face into the whirling, muck-encrusted blades—and up the back steps.

"Your mom's busy in the living room," the man said in his ear, tone friendlier than the circumstances warranted. "Don't want to bug her." He lowered his voice. "You LIKE bugging her, don't you?"

"No?"

The man shook him. "Don't lie to me. I see everything. I KNOW everything."

"Leave me alone!"

The man tucked Damien under his arm, easy as the morning paper, and opened the back door. "I'm going to make sure you never bother her again."

Damien tried to cry out, but the man squeezed him so tightly his yawp was born a wheeze.

And died on his lips.

"This way," Michaela said, then felt kinda dumb because OF COURSE their neighbor knew the way. The older woman didn't seem to notice, striding across the pavement with a macramé bag swinging from her shoulder, stuffed with all sorts of potions and powders and assorted gris-gris, the totems of a half-dozen religions the hippie had sampled like a tapas menu for most of her sixtyish years.

"Don't you worry, we'll get to the bottom of this," Zephyr said. "I'm very sensitive. Ever since I was a little girl, I saw things that other people couldn't. The world isn't what they say it is."

"Okay."

"You're lucky to have a neighbor like me. Round

here, all the Christians? They'd sprinkle your mother with holy water—" She gagged on her words, "—read some nonsense from that BOOK of theirs, and nothing would get done."

Michaela furrowed her brow—the Haskins family THOUGHT of themselves as Christian, but their particular breed of Christianity was vague, limp, a wet rag. Still, she felt a LITTLE insulted.

"I, on the other hand, have traveled the world, New Orleans, Jamaica—learning from the masters, those with intimate knowledge of what lies beyond the veil. And—"

"Just help my mom, okay?" Michaela said, mounting the curb. Sabrina was gone, the front door closed. The mower that had kicked off this latest meltdown still sat beside the house.

Zephyr nodded curtly. "I'll do my best."

Damien squirmed in his captor's embrace—many a time he'd pithily recited that old saw about the definition of insanity, doing the same thing over and over again, but his vaunted mind was no help, couldn't conjure up any novel solution to his predicament.

Bite, scratch, claw.

SCREAM.

The man dragged him down the hall—he caught a quick glimpse of Mom, squatting in front of the TV, caressing the static with her fingertips—then up the stairs.

Towards his parents' room.

MAN, FUCK THIS HOUSE

Damien smiled—the last part of his planned surprise. He sucked a breath in through his nostrils, tensed his muscles—

The man hit the tripwire. Immediately, two massive buckets of pig's blood doused them. Damien squeezed his eyes shut, tried not to gag on the rancid iron tang in the air—*all smells are particulate*—and wriggled against his captor's grip.

No use.

"Bleh," the man said, "that's nasty." Then he carried the bloodsoaked boy into the master bathroom like nothing had happened, nothing at all.

Hot water rushed from the spigots, filling the tub. Steam curled from the surface.

The man plopped down on the edge. Dipping his free hand in the water—he only needed one hamhock to hold the boy—he swirled it around, nodding to himself.

"Be full soon."

Damien peed.

A little.

No, a lot.

And then did a thing that the average ten-year-old did fairly frequently, though few would ever admit it.

He cried out for his mother.

On TV, DanKeith OlberHolt grinned and said, "So, I understand you've got some MAJOR NEWS regarding your #1 hit show, *Paying Heed to the Haskinseses.*"

"That's right, DanKeith." Screen-Sabrina nodded

at Screen-Perryman. "[Bleep] and I have been talking—"

DanKeith held up a finger. "Sorry to interrupt, but who exactly is [Bleep]?"

"Oh, [Bleep] is—I guess you could say he's our producer."

In the living room, Sabrina leaned forward on the couch, barely blinking, eyes bone-dry. Unaware she was chewing her nails to the quick.

"Should we tell them?" Screen-Sabrina said. "About the casting change?"

Screen-Perryman nodded vigorously, jowls bouncing up and down. "Go right ahead, Sabrina. After all—"

DanKeith, Screen-Sabrina and Screen-Perryman all leapt into the air simultaneously and froze, suspended above the stage, while the legend IT'S YOUR FAMILY smeared itself across the screen in a drippy, crimson font.

The studio lights darkened, the camera zoomed in on Screen-Sabrina. Solemn music played in the background.

"As you know," Screen-Sabrina said, a study in gravitas, "Damien hasn't been pulling his weight lately. He doesn't really add anything to the storyline. So, we're writing him off."

"Writing him off?" DanKeith replied, mock-shocked.

"That's right," Screen-Perryman said, nodding stoically. "If anything, he's a liability."

Blood from her chewed fingers dribbled down the corner of Sabrina's mouth, the words echoing in her head.

MAN, FUCK THIS HOUSE

Liability liability liability.

She saw the horned, capering, demonic creature that had chased her into the house, frothing at the mouth, ready to devour her very soul.

But she also saw the little boy underneath all that makeup—OBVIOUS makeup, she'd really thought him a demon? She saw the baby he'd been, the loquacious toddler, the curious and withdrawn boy he'd become. Sure, she didn't understand him, and yes, he certainly unsettled her.

Maybe he wasn't the child she'd dreamed of, and maybe the good Lord owed her another one. But at the end of the day, despite the half-finished pentagram scratched beneath her feet, the cheap Halloween get-up, all of it—

He wasn't a LIABILITY.

"He's my son," Sabrina whispered.

And then she heard it.

Her finally-acknowledged son, that bright, clever, diabolical little boy.

Screaming his bloody lungs out.

Michaela yanked on the front door. "It's stuck."

"Let me," Zephyr said, elbowing her aside. The older woman twisted the doorknob—nothing—then fiddled with Michaela's key. Still, the door wouldn't open.

Zephyr huffed, backed away, looking the door up and down. "It's shut us out."

"What's shut us out?"

"The house." Zephyr opened her bag, rummaged through the assorted vials. "When I came to visit your mother the other day, I felt it, but I had no idea, the power—" she trailed off, clinking glass speaking for her instead.

"What're we going to do?" Michaela asked, hugging herself. Something was very, very wrong—the hairs on the back of her neck stood tall, like in anticipation of a storm—but she couldn't fathom the precise nature of the disturbance.

Still, she couldn't help but wonder—Mom had claimed the house was haunted, and now their neighbor was speaking of the structure as if it had purpose, intention? How did that make sense?

Zephyr produced a jar of white powder from her bag— "Aha"—and twisted the cap free. She dumped the powder on the porch, chanting a hymn in some unknown tongue.

Unneeded, Michaela drifted over to the window, looked inside. Sabrina sat on the couch, enraptured by a static-spewing television, evidently chewing her fingers off.

"Mom!" she cried, banging on the window. "Mom, let us in!"

The old woman tapped on the window. "Sabrina? Hey, Sabrina!"

Sabrina sat bolt upright, not in response to their cries, but a scream coming from upstairs.

Damien.

Sabrina ran for the stairs. Michaela smacked the window again, but couldn't get her attention. What was going on in there?

Nothing good.

"We have to get inside," Michaela said, tugging on Zephyr's arm.

MAN, FUCK THIS HOUSE

"There's one last spell we can try. Find a rock. A big one."

Michaela ran down the steps—jumping over the last—and landed in the grass. The flagstone walkway seemed to fit the bill. She leaned down, prying a rock loose with her fingers—the squirming horrors underneath went unnoticed, as did the fresh mud staining her hands—and she carried it back up the steps, swaying under its weight.

Zephyr took the rock from her. "I hope you're not partial to that window."

She squared up with the window, rock raised overhead, chest heaving.

Michaela watched, pulse pounding.

"One," Zephyr said, "Two—"

The front door swung open, and Hal stuck his head out. "What in the world are you doing?"

Zephyr paused, rock held high. "Uh—"

Michaela, overcome with relief, rushed into the arms of her father. "Dad! When did you—"

"There, there," Hal said, patting her back while she hugged him tight. "Everything's going to be okay.

"Daddy's home."

Half-full.

The water ran, Damien struggled, but he was tired, so tired. Banging ineffectual fists against his mountainous abductor proved an ever-more-taxing chore. And the steam rising off the water—almost looked INVITING, now, didn't it?

Intellectually, he understood what was

happening. Whoever this man was, he seemed bent on drowning Damien in the bath.

And the more he sat there, tight in the man's grasp, the wet humidity of the room beading on his cheeks, the more he figured it didn't much matter at all. He'd fought with everything he had, and his efforts had been for naught. Why keep trying, then? Why waste the little energy he had left on a futile endeavor?

Damien had been a committed atheist for most of his life, except for a short Santa Claus-related dalliance, but even he could acknowledge his belief system was built on rationality, not direct knowledge. No one had direct knowledge of death except those who'd experienced it, and they remained famously tight-lipped about the whole thing.

No one's better at seeking out silver linings than the profoundly doomed.

"I tried to warn you," the man said. "Tried to make FRIENDS, even. First day you moved in, when you were out in the yard?"

The texts. Damien felt like a buffoon—assuming them some complicated sister-play, when in fact—

"Good enough," the man said. The spigots turned themselves off.

Damien didn't know whether the apparently supernatural feat made him more or less scared. His pulse said one thing, logic-brain said something else entirely. Any hint of the supernatural was very good news, for someone in his inescapable predicament.

"You're not human?" Damien said, less a question than a statement.

The man winked at him. "Human is as human does."

MAN, FUCK THIS HOUSE

And thrust him beneath the surface.

Hot water scoured Damien's skin. He tried to hold his breath, pushed on the sides of the tub, but an inexorable weight kept pressing him down, down, down—

He tried.

He really, really tried. But in the end?

He inhaled.

Back at the hospital, Detective Sherman was trying to rustle a bag of Doritos out of the vending machine when the nurse found her.

"Got those lab results on Haskins," the nurse said, handing her a print-out.

Sherman scanned it quickly. *PT/INR? Warfarin?* Haskins wasn't SUPPOSED to be on blood thinners. And, hypothetically speaking, if someone wanted to poison their spouse, like the nervous, aloof woman she'd just interviewed?

In addition to being a clinically prescribed anti-coagulant, warfarin was ALSO widely used as a rat poison. Sherman knew from experience that dosing was crucial—Haskins imbibed enough to kill a child, but not a slightly overweight, almost middle-aged man.

Common mistake.

She reached for her radio.

"What's going on here, kiddo?" Hal asked, ruffling Michaela's hair. The question was spoken to her, but he kept looking at Zephyr.

Still poised at the living room window with a heavy flagstone braced in her hands.

"Mom's acting weird, so I went to get Mrs. Zephyr—"

"Zephyr," Zephyr said, still not letting go of the rock.

"—and now the door won't open, and Mom won't let us in?" The rush of words ended, Michaela burrowed into her father's chest, glad HE was here, HE could deal with it.

Not her.

This wasn't her job at all.

Michaela's nose twitched. Her father usually smelled like some combination of Barbasol, Old Spice, and sweat. He smelled like SOME of those things now, but mostly?

He smelled like THEIR HOUSE.

"Drop the rock," Hal said.

"Look, Mr. Haskins—" Zephyr interjected.

"I said," Hal thundered, flinging Michaela aside, "—DROP THE G.D. ROCK!" He tromped up the steps.

Zephyr, still holding the rock, backed away, butting up against the porch swing, sending it in backwards in a lazy arc. "Mr. Haskins, I know we haven't officially met, but—"

Hal unleashed a vicious backhand, knocking the flagstone out of Zephyr's hands. It sailed over the porch railing, end-over-end, embedding in a patch of grass.

"DAD!" Michaela shouted, stunned by the sudden outburst.

Zephyr tried to back away, fell down on the porch.

Hal loomed over her, fists bunching.

Zephyr grabbed something from her pocket and threw it in his face—powder, like flour in an old *Three Stooges,* covered his cheeks, his chin.

Hal blinked.

Wiped a stripe across his eyes with a forearm.

And grabbed Zephyr by the hair.

Spitting white powder, Hal yanked, audibly tearing her brown-grey hair out at the roots. Zephyr wailed, grabbing his hand.

"Dad, stop!" Michaela shouted, but her feet were rooted in place.

Zephyr screeched, clawed, but Hal didn't seem to notice. He dragged her across the porch—by the hair—and threw her down the steps. The old woman tumbled ass-over-elbows, landing in a spindly, mewling pile.

"You don't even live in a real house," Hal said. He spat in the dirt next to Zephyr.

Zephyr pushed herself up to her hands and knees—blood trickled from her scalp—and pointed a gnarled, accusatory finger at Hal. "I know what you are." Her finger dipped down, scratching a quick pentagram in the dirt. She thrust her head back, arms outstretched, howling at the sky, "Before me, Raphael, behind me, Gabriel, at my right hand, Michael, at my left hand—"

Hal jumped off the porch, landing in the pentagram, a cloud of dust poofting up in his wake. He grabbed Zephyr again—by the throat, rather than the hair—cutting off her spell, her prayer. Her lament.

He cocked his head at Michaela. "Not much of a team player, is she?"

CRACK!

Hal lifted the woman easily, shook her limp body in the direction of her house— "Ha! How ya like that?"

Then dropped her in the dirt.

Michaela felt sick. She couldn't wrap her head around the fact that her dad—DAD—had attacked a woman, for no reason, and ki—ki—

She couldn't finish.

"How about some ice cream?" Hal said, wiping his hands on his jeans.

Michaela gaped at him, backed away, palms up. He looked exactly like her father, but something wasn't right. Not only his murderous behavior, either.

This wasn't her father.

Just a perfect copy.

Ignoring the dead woman on the ground—a moment she'd be rehashing with her therapists for the next thirty years—Michaela ran across the lawn towards the side of the house.

The thing, wearing her father's image like a perfectly-cut suit, thundered after.

She pumped her arms, legs churning against the turf, but he was faster, slamming into her. She cried out, flying across the lawn, lateralling into the mower. The handle slammed into her side—painfully—and she fell over.

Michaela landed on the grass, seeing stars, blinking at the late-afternoon sky.

Hal's grinning face filled her field of vision.

MAN, FUCK THIS HOUSE

Sabrina mounted the stairs, one-by-one, moving in a fog. At the landing she paused, momentarily forgetting herself. Admired the fine finish on the banister, so smooth she could slide right down it without ever worrying about an errant splinter getting stuck in her keister.

It really WAS a nice house, wasn't it?

Her bedroom door was open, the sound of the filling bathtub echoing. She walked slowly down the hall, a nagging feeling driving her, although she couldn't quite remember what it was. Something she'd seen on TV, but even though she'd just watched the program, the details had already faded from her mind.

The sound of running water abruptly cut off. She heard voices, talking to each other—one calm, collected, the other high-pitched, panicked.

Afraid.

Very, very afraid.

She burst through her bedroom door, nearly tripping on a pair of Hal's shoes he'd left next to the bed. A light was on in the master bathroom, steam wafting out the door.

"Hello?" Sabrina called, and instantly felt very, very stupid.

"In here," a voice said—amiable and familiar, like when she prowled their old house trying to find Hal, catching him at his workbench, tinkering with some fritzing appliance.

She entered, froze in the doorway, the odd tableau stopping her in her tracks like a taser.

The man from the Experience, the man who was currently in prison and in her house—the Simultaneous Man, one could call him—sat on the edge of the tub, casual, placidly grinning. One arm splayed across his knee, the other sunk in the bathwater up to the elbow, holding someone under.

Who for their part thrashed and kicked and splashed water all over the floor.

The tiny basketball sneakers—size 5, small for his age—told her precisely WHO was being drowned in her tub.

"Heeeey," Perryman said, casual as you please. "We're almost done here."

"What're you doing?" Sabrina managed.

"I told you, it'll be better without him around. I've seen the way he torments you."

"But, you can't—"

"I only want to make your life easier, Sabrina. I can take care of everything. I HAVE to, because no one else will."

The thrashing slowed. Sabrina felt sick to her stomach.

"No!" she screamed, charging. She rammed into Perryman, bouncing off, slamming painfully into the towel rack.

He wagged a finger at her. "Let me take care of this. He's been mean to you, and he did an awful, awful thing to me. You saw the living room. My beautiful floors!"

"Stop it!" Sabrina looked about for a weapon, anything. The welt on her back throbbed. She turned, grabbed the towel rack with both hands, and yanked it out of the wall.

"Ow, quit it!" Perryman cried, cringing.

The distraction was enough—Damien broke the surface, sucked in a desperate breath.

Before being pushed down again.

Sabrina summoned up every last bit of maternal strength she had and swung the towel rack at Perryman. The metal bar clunked off his forehead.

Perryman blinked. "That's not necessary."

Sabrina hit him again, and again, flailing away. The blows landed on his head, his broad brow, across his mouth.

Nothing.

Sabrina whirled and hit the wall, taking a chunk out of the drywall.

"Ouch!"

Again, Perryman's grip faltered, Damien snuck a breath.

Sabrina clutched the towel rod in both hands, reared back, plunged it into the wall. Gritting her teeth, she bore down, scoring a jagged, lightning strike slice in the drywall. Plaster dust erupted, a bitter, gritty cloud that scoured her throat, her nostrils.

"Stop," Perryman whined.

Sabrina dropped the towel rod, gripped the hole in the wall with both hands, tore a large chunk free.

"No!" Perryman hopped to his feet, grabbing her arms. He spun Sabrina around to face him, a pained expression on his face. "Please don't do that. I'm trying to help—"

A form erupted from the tub, splashing reddish water everywhere. Damien—soaking wet, makeup running down his face, a single, askew horn clinging stubbornly to his forehead—vaulted out of the tub, slipped on the wet floor, careened into the sink.

Perryman shoved Sabrina against the wall, moving faster than a man his size had any right, and lunged for Damien. He tackled him, football-style, wrapping the boy up in his arms. They both slammed into the cabinet, ripping it off the wall. Perfume bottles fell, shattered, effervescent clouds of fruity florality filling the steamy air.

Damien squirmed free, rolling in broken glass. Rivulets of blood ran down his face, his arms.

Perryman tried to grab his ankle, but the boy juked too fast, slipping out of his grip.

And running out the door.

His hands were on her.

Rough—these were not her father's hands at all, soft from years of office work. He grabbed her throat, squeezed the breath from her lungs.

Michaela panicked, raking his hands with her nails—small, paltry, cut to the quick because her parents wouldn't let her grow them out, not yet—but he didn't budge.

He just kept grinning.

"Come on, you're the GOOD one," Hal said, hot breath choking her as much as his hands, redolent of sawdust and mothballs and bleach. "Not like Damien. You're mommy's little angel, aren't you?"

But she wasn't, she'd never been. A daughter, yes. An angel?

Never.

Maybe soon, unless she did something.

MAN, FUCK THIS HOUSE

Later, she'd wonder why he didn't snap her neck like Zephyr's, and eventually find an answer she could live with, if not understand, in those words—*you're mommy's little angel.*

In the moment, she had no time to ponder.

Only act.

She got one hand under his fingers—vises, for sure—giving her room to breathe, while the other scrabbled above her head for a weapon, a rock, something she could bash into his daftly-grinning face and buy herself the time and space needed to escape.

Her fingers found the mower's pull-cord.

Instinctively, she yanked, the careened mower roared to life. The blades whirled, a great deathly gust ruffling her hair, whipping it across her face.

The Hal-thing cocked its head to the side, loosened its grip. "You want to help your dad with the grass? That's nice of you. See, I KNEW you weren't like the other one. You're a good little girl who does what she's told?"

Michaela sucked in a breath, her throat scratchy. She could barely hear him over the whup-whup-whupping mower, but nodded quickly—*I'm a good girl, yessiree.*

Hal backed off, sat on his haunches. "I'm so relieved. I really didn't want to—I don't LIKE doing this." He gestured around the front of the house, where Zephyr's body lay, unseen. "But when someone gets in the way, makes it hard for me, I have to—" he trailed off, shrugging, *what're you gonna do?*

Michaela squirmed out from under her father. She tried to look apologetic, wagged a fistful of loose hair at him. "I need a hair tie, then I'll help you with the grass?"

Hal grinned, clapped his hands. "That would be great! Team Haskins! Woooooooooo!"

Michaela stood, circled around him, unwilling to turn her back.

"Don't be too long," Hal said. "It's going to be dark soon."

"Be right back!"

Part of her wanted to run for the street, but she knew that would be useless. He'd catch her in a second, and though he seemed to possess a childlike, simplistic understanding of his world, she couldn't count on outwitting him again.

Then she saw it.

The flagstone, half-buried in the yard, one jagged end jutting up.

Michaela moved casually, like she was actually going to grab a hair tie, watching the Hal-thing from her peripherals. Her hands shook—could she really do this?

The spasm eased.

She could do this.

She HAD to.

In one quick motion, Michaela snatched up the flagstone—heavy, but like a feather in the hands of a desperate young girl—and turned, charging the Hal-thing, the stone clutched tightly to her chest.

Hal cocked his head to the side, rising—

Michaela hefted the rock like a chest-passed basketball. The stone caught the Hal-thing in the face, snapping his head around.

He fell, face-first.

Into the mower's rapidly spinning blades.

CRRRRRONCCCCH!!!!!!

MAN, FUCK THIS HOUSE

The Hal-thing's body jumped and spasmed as the blades tore through his face. He flailed, pushed at the mower. One hand got caught in the blades, then—

CLUNK, CLUNK, CLUNK.

The mower stopped.

The air smelled like burning metal. If the Hal-thing were human, the lawn should by all rights be covered in a spray of blood and gore, lacerated flesh, splintery bone chips.

But no—the detritus spewed across the lawn looked more like wood shavings and powdered drywall than anything that might have come from a human body.

Michaela gave the corpse a wide berth, inching over to the flagstone. Picked it up again, pressed the weight against her—comforting like a heavy blanket. She watched for any sign of movement, any hint the nightmare might not be over.

The Hal-thing stirred.

Michaela jumped back, unable to believe it. The body—that's what it was now, a BODY—twitched. Its undamaged hand pushed first at the mower's casing, then at the ground. Its head—what was left of it—wobbled from left to right, like a drunk trying to shake the cobwebs out.

"Oh no," Michaela muttered.

A noise, a wailing cry of—not exactly pain, but a close cousin—emerged from the creature's ruined mouth. It worked its way up to its knees.

Michaela, gripping the rock, moved behind it, trying to stay out of—view? Had it ever really SEEN, could it still?

A question for philosophers, should any take up

the case of the bizarre happenings at 4596 James Circle. Not little girls trying their level best to survive.

The wailing stopped. The Hal-thing pushed back up to its knees, one-handed—the other dangled at its side, shirtsleeve shredded at the wrist, lacerated wood and dangling wires poking out.

Michaela raised the stone above her head. She let out an animalistic squall and charged, ready to finish the job the mower started.

Then the Hal-thing turned, and the sight froze her in her tracks.

Damien ran.

Bloodied, heart pounding, gasping for breath, he mustered what strength he could and launched himself out of the bathroom, rocketing towards the bedroom door.

It slammed shut in his face.

Damien jumped back, bumped off his parents' bed. Grabbed the doorknob and twisted, but it held fast.

Perryman's large shape filled the bathroom doorway. "Get back here you little—ah!" Something shattered in the bathroom, he twinged in pain. "Please don't do that!"

Damien took advantage of the distraction and ran for the window, pushing it open. He tried to crawl out, but the window slammed shut, nearly severing his fingers.

Perryman roared, charging him. Damien ducked under the man's outstretched arms, seized a lamp off the nightstand—the plug offering the slightest resistance before coming free—and threw it at the window, hard as he could.

The window shattered, Perryman yowled.

Another loud crash from the bathroom—maybe the picture window by the tub, the mirror, something—and Perryman fell to his knees. Tears streamed down his big, ruddy face.

Sabrina appeared in the bathroom doorway, brandishing the towel rack like a sword. "Break something! Now!"

Damien grabbed the closest thing at hand—an end table—lifted it high, and slammed it into the floor. The legs splintered.

Perryman grinned.

"Not our stuff!" Sabrina cried. "Break THE HOUSE!"

Damien stared at her, confused, until Sabrina slammed the towel rod into the wall, lancing some very nice wallpaper.

Perryman fell back to his knees, hands covering his face.

They're connected.

Damien looked about something sturdy he could use to dig into the walls. Nothing.

Then a light breeze fluttered across his face.

Not from the window.

The ceiling fan.

Damien dodged another wild swing from Perryman and jumped on the bed—a child all over again—leaping for the ceiling fan.

Thankfully it was on the slow setting—he caught the fan blades on the first try. He spun around for a single, dizzying moment, soggy sneakers kicking out—

Though small for his age, the ceiling fan was made to hold no weight at all, even something so slight as an underweight 4D chess master like Damien Haskins.

The fan blades broke off in his hands.

Damien fell—not far—landing on the bed and bouncing off. His sneakers squelched when he hit the ground.

Perryman, who'd been rhinoceresing his way across the bedroom, suddenly seized up, like he'd thrown out his back, and fell to the ground.

"Go!" Sabrina said, tearing another chunk of drywall free, exposing studs and wiring and mouse turds. "Get out of here!"

Damien, still holding the fan blades—the fan itself hung limply from its wiring, an eye yanked from its socket—didn't move. "What about you?"

The pile of Perryman on the floor stirred, pushing up to his knees.

"I'll be fine, it's you he wants. Now go!"

Damien swallowed—she had a point. He clambered for the window, pushing through feet-first, cutting his palms open on the glass sticking out of the frame. Barely felt it. He hauled his small body through the aperture—the ground looked far, far away, even for an adult, but it beat drowning in the bathtub.

Perryman huffed with rage.

Sabrina tossed the towel rod on the comforter, climbed up on the bed, and grabbed the limply-hanging ceiling fan by its casing.

Perryman looked at her, at his original quarry hanging out the window, back again.

He took a single, heavy step in Damien's direction.

MAN, FUCK THIS HOUSE

"Mom?" Damien called.

"Jump!" Sabrina replied, yanking on the ceiling fan's motor for all she was worth.

Damien pushed himself away from the window, hanging motionless for what felt like an eternity.

Too late, it occurred to him there was something he really should have said.

"I love—" he called, as gravity bore both child and words away.

The Hal-thing, faceless, stared at her—his skin shorn off, revealing what should have been bone and tissue

But was not.

Michaela goggled, trying to make sense of the sight. The ragged rim of skin around Hal's face revealed an exposed 4x4, bristling with nails. Wiring, screws, an improbable mishmash of construction materials, dappled with drywall flecks like powdered sugar.

Hal took a staggering step towards her, dark brown clumps that looked like rat feces falling out of his face.

"You're no angel," he said, lipless, the words resounding from somewhere within his ruined face. "Look what you did to me! Look. What. You. DID!"

Michaela screamed, equally terrified by the sight and the pure, incandescent rage frothing forth from the Hal-thing. She raised the flagstone over her hand, hands shaking so badly she feared she'd smash her own skull open before the Hal-thing—*House-thing*—had a chance.

"Ahh!" she cried, heaving the stone.

It sailed through the air, slammed into the House-thing's torso. The House-thing tottered, took a step back—

And laughed, a dusty, echoing noise. The House-thing bent down, tried to pick up the flagstone one-handed, but only succeeded in tipping the stone over on its foot.

"Oh well," it said, righting itself. "I don't need that."

The House-thing rushed her, one hand outstretched, the other ruined appendage hanging at its side, frayed wires wiggling like earthworms—

BLAM! BLAM! BLAM!

Shots rang out, bullet holes erupted in the House-thing's shirt. The thing slowed, dust whooshed out of the wounds.

Michaela, ears ringing, turned and ran.

A woman in a brown pantsuit stood on their lawn, aiming a pistol at the House-thing, flanked by three other cops holding handguns. Two police cruisers, lights flashing, were parked in the street behind them at odd angles.

"Detective Sherman, Jackson Hill PD!" the woman cried. "Get DOWN, Michaela!"

Michaela had no time to wonder how the woman knew her name. She hit the deck—HARD—and pressed her hands over her ears as tightly as she could.

She still heard EVERYTHING, dozens of shots, too many to count.

Someone picked her up, and then she was moving, the world swaying wildly around her. For a moment she feared the House-thing had gotten hold of her, but the person smelled like a man, aftershave and sweat, and she could see his blue uniform, hear the radio hissing in her ear.

They reached a patrol car. Her savior wrenched the back door open, shoved her inside, then shut the door.

Michaela twisted around in the seat, trying to see, but the cop backed up against the window. More shots rang out, he reloaded, then advanced again, firing quickly.

Despite herself, Michaela pressed up against the glass to see what was going on.

The House-thing—bullet-ravaged—teetered across the lawn. Sherman barked orders, popped off a few shots, ejected her clip and slammed a new one home in a single, smooth motion.

One of the other cops broke away, running for the cruiser. Michaela thought he was going to drive her away—and how COULD he, her mother was still inside, not to mention her brother—but he angled around to the trunk.

Came back into view a second later.

Racking a shotgun.

He yelled something—Michaela could hear very little through the glass—and tossed the gun to Sherman. She dropped her pistol, caught it, whirled around to face the House-thing, now only feet away.

She aimed at a knee and fired both barrels.

The buckshot tore the House-thing's leg in half, instantly dropping it. The cops circled it, still pumping bullets.

But it didn't rise again.

The ankle broke his fall.

Wait, that wasn't right.

The FALL broke his ANKLE.

He might have hit his head, too, but that was a far less pressing concern. His foot was twisted at a weird angle. What novelty! He'd never supposed an ankle could bend THAT way.

Damien's logic-brain realized he was being a bit TOO magnanimous about his ankle, determined he must be in shock, and crawled away from the gods-cursed house before the pain—surely coming soon, and with a vengeance—made him black out.

He inched across the grass, pleasantly surprised by his pace—maybe he should crawl EVERYWHERE, to the bus stop, Mr. Tuthill's class, the bathroom and the principal's office and everywhere else he ever had to go.

Then the air erupted with gunshots.

LOTS of gunshots.

Yelling, too, snatches of undecipherable orders or anger in between fusillades. Damien had no idea what they were talking about, or what they were shooting AT for that matter. The smart move was usually to crawl AWAY from the gunfire, but he was pretty sure they said something about POLICE.

The gunfire stopped. Grass-stained, wet, and bloody, Damien rounded the house and saw four police officers huddled over something on the front lawn, firearms at the ready.

Thinking quickly, he broke off the last horn on his

head and tossed it away, then pushed himself up into a seat.

"Over here!" he cried, waving his hands.

One of the cops holstered their pistol and sprinted across the lawn. "I've got you," the cop said, picking Damien up with ease.

He shivered, reminded of the way Perryman grabbed him.

The cop asked him his name, told him he was very brave—Damien found it a bit patronizing—and hauled him over to a cruiser. Michaela waited inside, face and fingers pressed up against the window. She scooched away when the cop opened the door, planted him on the seat.

"We'll take a look at that ankle in a sec, hold tight for me, okay?" The cop thumbed his radio, barked something about EMS and where the EFF were they?

Michaela hugged Damien tightly. "My God, are you okay?"

"I think so—" He leaned out of the car, head swimming, nearly falling over into the street. "My mother's still in there," he said, pointing up at the house.

The man said *watch your legs* and shut the door.

And then they were alone.

"What happened?" Michaela asked, still clinging to him fiercely.

Damien looked to their house, searching for clues in the windows. "I honestly have no idea."

Even in her college days, Sabrina had never, ever wrecked a house, outside of the occasional broken beer bottle, or the time some spindly sub-IKEA kitchen chair collapsed under her weight in front of all her friends, to her horror.

Now she was making up for lost time.

With Damien out the window, the fight seemed to leave Perryman. He cowered in the corner, pleading with her to stop.

She did not.

Sabrina liberated one of Hal's golf clubs from his closet—a far better tool than the towel rod—and got to work smashing windows, shattering the sink in the kids' bathroom, knocking shower heads to the ground.

Perryman crawled down the hall after her, on his knees, begging.

She ignored him, instead rearing back and cracking the tile. Then she turned the faucets on full-blast, swung at the pipes underneath the sink—one, two, three times—knocking them loose. Water rushed out, the jet soaking the bathroom.

Perryman made no effort to stop her. He lay splayed across the hardwood floor in the hallway, one arm reaching pitifully, the other twisted beneath his bulk.

Sabrina cracked a few more divots in the drywall. But what was she doing, tearing the murderous house down by hand? Silly and impractical, when she could just douse it in gasoline—there was a Texaco down the street, she could be there and back in minutes.

Sabrina nodded to herself. She'd been flailing, striking out in desperation and anger. But this, this was calculated. She was in control.

Then Perryman started melting into the floorboards.

Slowly, his skin lost its consistency, features distorting, melting like candlewax. Inch by inch, his body sucked into the floor.

Reabsorbed by the house.

And if that weren't horrible enough, the floor suddenly tilted on its axis, sending her flying down the hall.

Fire trucks, sirens blaring, filled the cul-de-sac, followed by ambulances. Damien and Michaela watched from the back of the police cruiser. Two firefighters hopped off the truck, had a quick conference with the police—they were still huddled around the House-thing, or what was left of it, unwilling to point their weapons away, disbelieving a threat such as that could ever truly be vanquished— and then Detective Sherman broke away, opened the cruiser door.

"They're going to look at you in a second," she said, speaking to both Haskins children, gesturing at some EMTs piling out of an ambulance. Several firefighters wearing breathing apparatus and carrying axes were heading up the lawn, flanked by the other cops.

"You're going to get my mom out of there, right?" Damien said. At his side, he could sense Michaela's sharp intake of breath at his words.

My mom.

"Why we're here," Sherman said with a tight smile. "Your dad's test results—we just want to talk to her, okay?"

"Where IS my dad?" Michaela asked.

Sherman narrowed her eyes. "Something he ate didn't agree with him. He's in the hospital, but he's okay."

Michaela breathed a sigh of relief.

"So, uh—you kids have any idea what's going on around here?"

Michaela shrugged, Damien shook his head.

"Maybe a gas leak. Gotta be, right?" Sherman said. She cast a look over her shoulder at the thing on the lawn. "Gas leak."

The EMTs were approaching, both carrying red plastic tackleboxes.

Sherman stood, patting the roof of the cruiser. "I'm going to find your mom, and then—"

GRRRRRRRRRRRRRRRRUNNNNNNNNNNNN NNNNNNNNNNNNNNN!

A loud noise rent the air, the ground quaked. Damien craned his neck around the detective to see what was happening.

Their house was crooked.

Canted, at an angle. It rocked back the other way, like a boat in rough seas. The air filled with a loud thrumming noise that rattled his teeth, bethrobbed his eyeballs. The house shifted one way again, then the other, the roof swinging wildly.

And then the house rose.

An impossible sight, surely, and maybe the cop was right about a gas leak, one so virulent the errant carbon monoxide Swiss-cheesed Damien's brain.

MAN, FUCK THIS HOUSE

But no. This was real.

The house STOOD on four concrete pillars—LEGS—dirt raining down from where it had ripped free of its moorings. A structure in flux, some walls contracted while others expanded, windows shattered, raining glass down on the cops and firefighters who'd been preparing to make entry, and were now either frozen in place or running for their lives.

The house's transformation completed in an instant, morphing from a run-of-the-mill Craftsman to a mutated beast Mr. Gustav Stickley could NEVER have envisioned, no matter how much laudanum he dropped. Balanced now on four legs, the house—the HOUSE—looked like something the Power Rangers might square off against. Some square footage had been repurposed into what looked like arms, hanging at the sides, one *fist* crowned with the chimney, the other made from aluminum siding.

The front door banged open, and a bestial howl emerged, one that shook the cop car on its suspension, nearly bowling Sherman over.

The howl died out, and for a moment, all was silent.

"MAN, FUCK THIS HOUSE!" one cop yelled, and fired indiscriminately at the Haskins home.

The House roared again, advanced across the yard, its four concrete feet punching holes in the grass. A firefighter tripped, was crushed. One of the remaining cops whirled and fired a few shots, but the house swung its chimney arm, hitting him so hard he sailed across the street and landed somewhere behind Zephyr's.

Presumably splattered like an insect.

Sherman barked commands into her radio, calling for backup from both the local PD and God himself. The House swatted another officer, crushing his arm, jagged bone slicing through his uniform sleeve. He slipped, firing with his good hand. A stray bullet caught Sherman right in the face. One second she was standing next to them, then her head snapped back, blood misting the window.

"Come on, we have to go," Michaela said, yanking Damien's sleeve.

He turned to look at her, amazed his sister could be so calm in the face of, of—all this. Of course he couldn't know she'd already grappled with impossibility once that afternoon, gazed right into its lawnmower-bitten face. But she seemed so self-possessed, and he was so confused, Damien knew there was only one option that made sense.

To trust in her completely.

"Let's go."

Michaela crawled over him—carefully—since the other door was locked, extended a hand. "Here, lean on me." He threw his arm around her shoulders, let her help him to his one good foot. They turned, together, like late entrants to the three-legged race at Field Day.

The House's shadow loomed large over them.

The Haskins children—conjoined—stared up at the 2,000-square foot monstrosity blocking out the sinking sun, the sky, EVERYTHING.

Too shocked to even scream when its concrete feet stamped down.

MAN, FUCK THIS HOUSE

The House, for the first time in its existence, left James Circle.

Left plenty of smoking wreckage in its wake, too—crushed police cars and upended emergency vehicles belched black smoke into the sky, flames licked the roofs of the neighboring houses. Smears on concrete marked lives lost, severed body parts lay about like cast-off children's toys, the sort of annihilation one might expect from a plane crash or meteor strike.

All soon forgotten.

The world the House entered was at once familiar and exhilaratingly new. Having spent the last twenty years observing its residents, ever since the slow rot of sentience crept into its once-inert frame, it had an idea of what Jackson Hill and the rest of the world was like—mainly from television, a genius invention that taught it so much. And yet there are certain things one can only know, down to one's studs, through experience.

Freed of its moorings, the House intended to have PLENTY of experiences.

Moving fast for a 400,000-pound structure on a concrete foundation repurposed into makeshift legs, the House turned right onto the main road, proceeding in a direction it hoped would take it to town, a place it had always been curious about. Humans liked to "eat," "drink," "shop"—all things one could do IN TOWN, the House learned over thousands of hours watching its occupants watch TV. Perhaps it could find similar delights—the House adored having its hallways swept, its plumbing snaked, gutters unclogged. When a cleaning crew Swiffered its floors, a slight giggle shivered through its frame.

And, truth be told, there was nothing quite like having a fresh coat of paint slapped on. Made the House feel new all over again.

Especially after the attack by its current owner—its insides felt raw, wind whistled through broken windows.

Per its TV watching, Jackson Hill did in fact have a paint store—Roy G's. The House paused in the middle of the street, trying to recall its location. Oncoming cars first honked their horns and then drove headlong into trees, tossing their owners through the windshields to break their necks on the forest floor.

Unfortunately, no one had ever thought to broadcast a map of Jackson Hill, so the House had no way of knowing where it was. No matter—it would simply walk down the road until it found the paint store, and by then perhaps it would have enough power to reconstitute some unused innards into an avatar that could speak for it, explain exactly what the proprietor of the paint shop needed to do.

Upon pain of death.

For it was tired of playing nice with humans. Yes, it owed its existence to them—if not for the resident Perryman's neglect, then the House wouldn't have needed to come alive to take care of itself.

But now, after the Haskins woman's betrayal—it was only trying to HELP, why couldn't she see that?

Well, the joke was on her. Her monster child was

currently smeared all over its feet, the woman herself asleep in its belly.

Hopefully gripped by the night terrors she deserved.

Sabrina woke up, not IN bed, but underneath it.

The last thing she remembered was hurtling down the hallway, the doorframe to their bedroom closing in at an alarming rate. She blinked, staring up at the underside of the box spring—the side of her face throbbed, a fat knot forming at her temple. She figured she must have glanced off the doorframe, then either crawled under the bed or been tossed there, by the—

Earthquake?

But it wasn't an earthquake, because even the most vigorous tectonic activity couldn't make a house move like THAT.

It occurred to her the house was still moving, the air filled with groans and crashes.

A nauseating feeling gripped her. Sabrina swallowed her gorge and crawled out from under the bed, grabbing the bedpost to keep from falling over. The floor rocked to and fro, sending end tables and lamps sailing from one side of the room to the other. All the lights were out, the room lit solely by the fading sun. The blown-up Sears portrait of the whole family hung askew, but still clung to the wall. Everything else was in such a shambles, it looked like a gang of particularly slovenly thieves ransacked the house.

Almost made the broken ceiling fan and the holes torn in the drywall look chic in comparison.

An image of her—not *her,* Screen-Sabrina—flashed through her mind, giving that one couple from the fixer-upper show a tour of their house, what were their names, Chet and Julia?

"Open walls are the new open floor plan!" Julia said brightly, then flipped open a box cutter and slit her husband's throat.

The house bucked, sending her into the bedpost. Sabrina winced, shaking off the pain. Pushed off, launching herself over to the broken window, to see what in the world was going on.

They were no longer on James Circle, that was for sure. Instead, the house seemed to be barreling down an unfamiliar road. Several crashed cars smoked, orange fire blazed off in the woods. The perspective of looking out her bedroom window and seeing the terrain PASS BY nearly broke her mind.

Like so many other experiences over the last few days.

Sabrina thought about jumping, but velocity and height—her second-floor bedroom towered more like THREE stories off the ground, somehow—stopped her. Visions of falling out the window, twisting in mid-air, snapping her neck against the asphalt bloomed in her mind.

No, jumping was out.

But what should she do instead?

She smacked the window frame with the flat of her hand in frustration. No response from the house, just a stinging palm. She sank to her knees, overcome.

Maybe she should crawl back under the bed, nod

off to sleep, wake up to find this was all a horrible dream, they were back in Columbus, stupid HAL had never packed up the family and forced them to move to this awful place after all. She shut her eyes tightly, covered her face.

"Stop!" Sabrina cried, desperation ratcheting her voice up to a shriek. "Will you STOP!"

The house did.

She opened her eyes. The room was still, the awful cracking, crashing, grinding sounds ringing in her ears. Carefully, she pulled herself up and looked out the window.

The house had come to a halt. In the middle of the freeway, sure, but it wasn't moving.

Thank the Lord for small miracles.

Speaking of miracles—Damien had jumped out the window, hopefully to safety, but Michaela—

Where WAS Michaela?

"Michaela?" she called, gingerly crossing to the bedroom door. "Damien? Anyone?"

No answer.

She grabbed another of Hal's golf clubs, stepped into the hallway. The spot where Perryman melted into the floor was indistinguishable, bore no sign anything extraordinary happened there. If not for the vista out her bedroom window, she might've shrugged, decided she'd gone insane, and headed down to the kitchen to fix herself a snack. She couldn't remember the last time she'd eaten, but she wasn't hungry. Wasn't ANYTHING but confused, tired, and so, so ready for life to go back to normal.

Sabrina crept down the hall, golf club at the ready, poking her head into the other rooms. She tried the light switches, but nothing worked. Other than the whole house looking like it had been turned upside down and given a vigorous shake, she didn't see anything out of the ordinary.

But the light was fading, and she didn't want to think about what might be swimming in the pools of shadow in the corners of the rooms.

Down the stairs, slowly, carefully. Sirens wailed in the distance—part of her hoped they were coming for her, but another part wondered what the authorities of the world might hope to do about something so clearly not beholden to any natural law she'd ever heard of.

What could they do? Call the army? Fight her HOUSE like Godzilla?

The thought of bomber jets soaring overhead, loosing missiles, spurred her to action.

Sabrina poked her head into the living room—the TV was off, at least. She tried the front door, but it wouldn't open, neither would the back. The faint scent of gas lingered in the kitchen.

The whole house GROANED, like it was caught in a storm, a hurricane gust rattling the siding. The floor lurched under her feet, Sabrina grabbed a burner for support.

And then, once more—

They were moving.

The kitchen bounced up and down. Cabinets yawned open, disgorging porcelain and cutlery. Dishes shattered, knives tumbled across the floor. A never-used blender—a long-ago wedding gift—struck the refrigerator, leaving a Vitamax-shaped ding in the door.

MAN, FUCK THIS HOUSE

Also: a pizza box flew off the counter, splatted on the ground, the lid bouncing up and down to the rhythm of the house's movement, a yawning puppet mouth laughing at her.

The legend on the lid read MORIO'S.

The pizza no one ordered—a first attempt by the house at ridding Sabrina, and itself, of Damien and maybe Michaela too?

Probably.

Gave her an idea.

The whole time she was fighting for Damien's life, Perryman—the House, that's who he was—never actually HURT her. Damien, yes.

But Sabrina herself?

Not really, though he could have. Kind of like what Zephyr'd said, after their first visit. The House could be scary, inscrutable, ludicrous—

But always trying to HELP her, wasn't it?

The House pushed its pace as fast as a mid-century Craftsman could. Sabrina had stopped ripping its guts out, so that was good—the damage was minimal, easily repaired, especially with fresh resources from the paint store.

If only it could repair its relationship with its owner.

The House felt her confusion, her anger, sitting in the kitchen like a rock in its stomach. Why couldn't she SEE? It only wanted to help her, and now, now—

Now, it had done a thing no house ever should.

Parted with its land? Rebelled against its owner? Run rampant?

Houses killed people all the time. Railings collapsed, outlets sparked, gas leaks pumped carbon monoxide.

And children died in bathtubs. Oh yes, they did.

The House remembered a television show—some news report. *Children can drown in as little as two inches of water.*

So why had it waited for the tub to fill?

The action made no sense, no sense at all. It could have drowned the child—or snapped his neck—and been done with it. And yet, it had waited. Waited until the Owner had come upstairs—it thought of Sabrina as the Owner, because houses knew nothing of deeds and property records, and like a parent, flush with secret shame, it always loved one resident best. Maybe that's why it had approached things the way it had, because it knew—deep in its bones—it had no hope of keeping her love.

It never had—never ever ever—in its long, long history.

But maybe—maybe it could try. Talk to her, in a voice she'd understand, though it wasn't ready, no, not quite...

Night was falling—a boon. The House continued along the road, looking for lights on the horizon, a hint it was headed in the right direction. Minutes more, and maybe it would turn, head back the way it came.

Sirens howled in the distance, and while the House knew what that meant, the people in the coming police cars could not know what they faced.

Every nail in the House's structure quivered in anticipation—still so long, it CRAVED battle, a chance to smash and destroy the things that ran through its guts like parasites, taking taking taking and never—

The House came to a stop, once again.

In the kitchen, the Owner dangled a slice of pizza over her open mouth.

Tongue stretched out to taste the poison.

Sergeant Toby O'Rourke listened to the squad room radios squawking and wondered if he were going insane.

His father had—cop also, nineteen years on the beat back in Chicago. Pulled the pin early after something happened he never talked about. Thought some mountain air would do him good, moved the whole family to Jackson Hill and got a job as a security guard at a local distribution center. Didn't help. Night terrors, random delusions, a whole protracted episode where he kept burying his wife's shoes in the backyard, putting tiny little popsicle-stick crosses on each "grave," magic marker-scrawled with symbols that made no sense to anyone, let alone Toby Sr.

Ate his gun three months later. Toby the younger, in high school at the time, finished growing up without a father and with the knowledge that deep within his DNA, he carried things he'd rather not.

When the initial reports came in, he blamed the messengers—pranksters, lunatics, whatever. Garden variety nutcases dialing 911 because a sasquatch ran through their backyard.

Allegedly.

The calls routed from dispatch, motorists who claimed to see a HOUSE rampaging down the road, he could dismiss those, laugh them off as acid freaks burning out their own brain cells on high-test Ellis Dee. But when his own officers called in—hesitant, like they knew they were lying—talking nonsense about James Circle, the poster child for bland suburbia?

Sergeant O'Rourke figured HE was the common denominator, and that didn't bode well, not at all.

Then his cell phone beeped.

Hand shaking, O'Rourke pulled the phone across his desk. He didn't want to look, he couldn't keep mainlining all this insanity. But maybe it was somebody level-headed like Casella, an old-timer with more hash-marks on his sleeve than O'Rourke himself.

Yeah, that was the ticket. Whatever was going on, one of the old vets was about to set everything right with an utterly mundane explanation. Maybe some drunk DUI'ed their way into the closest cell phone tower, and—cut off from Instagram, Twitter, blasted TIKTOK—the local residents had gone plumb crazy, started imagining things.

O'Rourke took a deep breath and checked his messages.

A video—from Casella—complete with running commentary.

"—didn't think you'd believe me, otherwise—BACK UP!" The video turned sideways, gunshots ringing out BAM! BAM! BAM!

Then the video ended.

O'Rourke sat back in his chair, nodding to himself.

MAN, FUCK THIS HOUSE

No prank, this. Unless it was a prank played by God on Man, and that was about the only thing that halfway made sense.

O'Rourke did two things in quick succession.

First, he called the National Guard down in Portales. Wouldn't do much good without the Governor, but that was a number he did not have. Best he could, he explained the situation to the disbelieving Guardsman on the other end. Got a cell number, forwarded the video. That would have to do.

Second, he drew his service weapon, put the barrel to his temple, and pulled the trigger.

Quivering in fear, shock, desperation, Sabrina held the cold, greasy, slice of pizza to her mouth and hoped the House would notice.

It did.

The House stopped, tossing her roughly against the stove—one more bruise on a body covered in them.

Sabrina rubbed her side with one hand, wincing.

It worked.

Maybe she wouldn't have to tear the house apart with her bare hands. Maybe—

The oven door banged open forcefully, cracking Sabrina a good one across her knee. She yelped, fell on her butt. The slice of pizza fell from her hands, slid across the floor. She reached for it—

And froze.

Something crawled out of the oven.

Sabrina couldn't see much in the gloom—a tumble

of lank hair, pale hands clasping either side of the oven, pulling itself into the world.

It scared her in a way even the initial specter of Dirk Perryman had not.

Sabrina pushed herself up, backing away, still-oily fingers held out to ward off whatever approached.

Halfway out the oven, the thing abruptly thrust its head up, hair flipping back over the stovetop, revealing its face. Queer, malformed—holes for eyes, a nub of a nose, skin like plaster in both color and affect. It opened its mouth—seven, eight teeth—and, voice raw, unfinished vocal cords working overtime to approximate a semblance of human speech—

Spoke.

"Sabrina." Voice like a rush of wind rustling grass grown over an unmarked grave.

Sabrina backed into the door that used to go to the backyard, and now presumably emptied out into—wherever they were. Her hand found the knob, turned.

Locked.

"Get away!" Sabrina hissed.

The creature tumbled out of the oven, looking like a bundle of rags on the kitchen tiles. Drew itself up on unsteady legs—Bambi on an ice patch. Its hand—three fingers, one more suggestion than digit—grabbed the counter, steadying itself.

"I was making this," the creature wheezed, every word a labor.

"Making what?"

The creature waved its hand from chin to groin, indicating itself.

"Why?" Sabrina said—stalling for time, still trying

to turn the knob, not caring if she tumbled out onto the highway and broke into pieces.

"So we could talk." The creature's nub of a nose pushed—slowly—out of its face, becoming ever more refined, its eye sockets filled with sclera, then—dear God—irises? Yes, irises. "I learned to make from watching. Watching you."

Sabrina kicked the back door. It didn't budge. "Talk about what?"

The creature rubbed its face, massaging its cheeks, temples, jawline. Its features—formerly blank—slowly took shape.

Sabrina felt sick—she knew exactly who the thing was trying so hard to imitate.

"This form," the creature said, "You spend so much time looking at it, in the mirror—I thought it might hold your attention." The creature's hands fell away from its face.

Sabrina Haskins stared back at herself. An imperfect likeness—hurried, the House had forgotten the light scar under her right eye from a nasty college-era fall, and the tone and texture of her hair seemed off—but otherwise it was a decent facsimile. Maybe not good enough to fool Hal, or Michaela or even Damien, but a stranger?

At a minimum, they'd think the thing was actually human.

Sirens grew louder in the distance. What would they do? What could they do?

Sabrina didn't want to be inside when they arrived.

"Let me go," Sabrina said.

Her doppelganger shook its head, once.

"I said, LET ME GO!" Sabrina threw herself upon the creature. One of its arms snapped in half—in its rush the House had clearly skimped on its own construction. The creature screamed, a broken two-by-four sticking out of its shoulder, another on the floor, crowned by a pale, clasping hand.

Sabrina burst into the foyer. The front door was still locked—of course—but the door to the basement?

Hoping against hope, Sabrina clasped the handle. And TURNED.

The door swung open. Without a thought, Sabrina rushed down the stairs. One, two—

Her third step hit empty space.

Her stomach lurched, she fell for the briefest of moments, free—

Before something grabbed her.

Sabrina's legs dangled over the road. The basement stairs she'd been descending ended, the basement itself left behind in the House's hurry to get away. Twelve, fifteen feet?

A painful fall, sure. But survivable.

Sabrina dug her nails into the arm across her chest, but the creature pulled her back up the abbreviated staircase. She thrashed, kicked—a shoe flew off, circling like a helicopter until it touched down on the double-yellow line below.

Groaning with effort, the creature wrenched her up the steps, depositing her on the hallway floor. Sabrina cried out, tried to lunge past it—

The creature kicked the door closed.

"Wasn't an exit, before," the creature said, tapping the door with its one remaining palm, smiling almost apologetically.

MAN, FUCK THIS HOUSE

Blue and red lights flickered in the living room windows.

"Let me go!" Sabrina cried, grabbing the creature—HER—by the throat. She squeezed, the flesh yielding—the "neck bone" would snap as surely as its arm did, oh yes it would—

"One question," the creature wheezed. "One question and I'll let you go."

Sabrina stopped squeezing, but didn't let up on the pressure already applied. "What?"

"When you first saw me—" the creature's voice was nearly a whisper, so constricted was its imitation airway, "—what did you think?"

"What?"

"The day you moved in. What did you think? How did you feel?"

"It doesn't matter." Sabrina squeezed harder—wood cracked beneath her fingers. A little more pressure and then—

"Please," the creature whispered, and Sabrina made the mistake of looking in its eyes—eyes so much like hers, and her own haggard, sweating image reflected back in the pupil.

Sabrina, on Sabrina, on Sabrina.

A Moebius strip of womanhood, real and fake intertwining.

Along with their fear, their pain. THEIRS.

"You the house!" squawked a bullhorn-enhanced voice from outside. "Uh, you IN the house. Put down, uh. Don't move!" Voices shouted commands, car doors slammed.

"I felt," Sabrina managed, mind drifting back to that long-ago Saturday when she'd first laid eyes on

4596 James Circle, "Happy. Like, like I'd found my dream home."

The Faux-Sabrina smiled wistfully. "I'm glad. You can feel that way again."

That way. The way she'd felt had been a lie. Why would she want to feel like THAT?

And then they were walking, hand-in-hand, through the house. Both Sabrinas—the other restored, or fully-formed, each wearing a cashmere sweater, jeans, fingers and wrists dripping with gold and silver. Day, now, motes of dust twinkling in windowlight, the only noises from outside the happy chirp of birds. The hallways were clean, and smelled of oak and pine, potpourri, muffins baking in the oven.

Blueberry?

Oh, yes.

All the good things.

"Where—"

"This is what could be," Faux-Sabrina said. "With you inside, all things are possible. You—" She grabbed Sabrina by the shoulders, peering deeply into her eyes. "You're all I've ever wanted. Someone to love me the way I love them. To care for me, to wax my tiles, wash my baseboards. Clean the gutters when they're full up with leaves. Polish me, paint me, fix me. For a long time, I was alone, worse—neglected. The old owner—Perry-Man—he wouldn't do anything. Left his trash everywhere. Raged against the world, broke windows, punched holes in my walls, let his friends do as they please. Cruel, so cruel, and no one did anything.

"So I did.

"I only wanted to be a house, not this, but—I

watched him, Perry-Man, and made a better version. Someone to do all the things he wouldn't. Eventually, the police came and took him away, and I was glad for it. Maybe I damned myself—what is a house without a resident—but I couldn't help it. I'd rather be empty, not full up with, with—"

Faux-Sabrina trailed off, tears welling in her eyes.

Sabrina's instincts kicked in, she patted the other woman's wrist—immediately forgetting she was talking to a house made up to look like HER in a dream. "I'm sorry that happened to you."

The House hugged her fiercely, chest heaving against her own. "Thank you."

Sabrina patted her back. "I see now. What you were trying to do—"

"I never wanted to scare you—"

"I know, I know."

And God help her.

She DID.

Zephyr was right—all the House ever seemed to do was help. Carrying boxes, brewing coffee. Sometimes it went too far, like with Hal—that was the House, wasn't it—or with Damien.

Which, if Sabrina really tried to put herself in the House's place, made at least a little bit of sense. It simply didn't know any better.

"I wish you could stay inside forever," the House said, tears running freely now. "I've been so empty."

"I know," Sabrina said softly. "But I've got to get back—"

She paused, mid-sentence.

Did she? Did she really?

Michaela was one thing, but Hal? A guy she

nominally loved, but she never picked too hard at her feelings for him, did she? And Damien, the little monster. Maybe she didn't want him DEAD, but—

And that vision, of what could be?

Blueberry muff—

The world shimmered, then they were back. The House was in a state, someone outside shouted into a bullhorn. The interior so dark Sabrina could hardly see the House-Her, mere inches away.

Sabrina went to the window. A half-dozen police cars were parked across the road—spike strips? Who thought SPIKE STRIPS might help—set up, a dozen cops hunkered down behind open cruiser windows, guns trained on the House. A glance through the rear windows showed the road behind them similarly blockaded.

But the sides of the road?

Empty.

The police never trained for anything like this, clearly.

"Run," Sabrina said.

"What?"

She motioned to the kitchen window. "Over the hills, far away. Otherwise, they'll destroy you. Bullets will rip you apart. And it's only a matter of time before they bring in the Army. Their bombs?"

The House regarded her for a long, long moment. "Then I'll be alone. Maybe better, better to—end things."

Sabrina pulled her close again. "You really were a great House. The best House." And it was true. Despite everything, as a HOUSE—

MUCH nicer than their place back in Columbus.

MAN, FUCK THIS HOUSE

"Fire on my command," the bullhorn voice said. "Ready—"

The basement door swung open.

"You can leave," the House said. "Crawl down the steps, run away. Go back to your family, and—find a new house. Love it like you loved me."

"I will," Sabrina said, tears welling in her own eyes now. She paused at the top of the stairs, a short jump to freedom. "I'll never—"

Bullets ripped through the front door, the back, the walls, punching through glass and wood and aluminum siding. One caught Sabrina in the leg, above the knee.

Another hit her in the throat.

Sabrina fell, blood gurgling from her mouth, too shocked to feel pain, or anything at all. Not even surprise. Darkness drew in from the edges of her vision.

The last thing she saw was herself, bent over her dying form.

Weeping tears like she'd never cried, never in life.

The barrage shattered windows, swiss-cheesed doors and walls. Bullets thunked into cabinets, sinks, floors. The gutters fell, hanging down the side of the house like a loose strand of hair.

The House howled in pain, fury. But it did not strike out.

It ran, fast as its concrete legs could carry it, across the fields, over the hills, and far away. Out of Jackson Hill, out of New Mexico, into the realm of dream and myth, of whispers and lies, another uniquely American anomaly.

Bigfoot? Champy? The World's Biggest Ball of Twine?

And the House.

Lost somewhere to the wilds that still exist, that we think we've conquered. But not alone.

Never alone.

Things were quiet, and then they were loud, and a fireman wrenched open the door of the crumpled-up police cruiser with the jaws of life. The Haskins children were birthed again into a world of light and sound and confusion, they held each other tightly, fighting any emergency personnel who tried to peel them apart to check for signs of injury.

There were none.

The Haskins children were whole, in body if not in mind. Eventually someone put two and two together, drove them to the hospital, ushered them into Hal's room.

"Hey, champ," Hal said, awake but weak, stinking like hospital food, lightly punching each of his children on the shoulder.

Tearful, they collapsed into his arms, and stayed like that for a very long time. Breathing as one.

Waiting for news of the fourth of their number.

Knowing in their hearts it would never come.

FRIDAY

DR. VICTOR GRAIS, part-time medical examiner and full-time golf cheat, entered the break room in the belly of Jackson Hill Presbyterian and groaned heavily. Bad enough he'd been called in this late, but SOMEBODY neglected to refill the coffee pot. A sludgy brown patina gathered at the bottom of the carafe, a sticky reminder of the boundless inconsideration of his fellow man.

Or something, he always waxed philosophical when he was exhausted or trying to impress a divorcee.

Grumbling over the city council's refusal to budget a proper assistant for him, Dr. Grais brewed a new pot since he was looking at an all-nighter.

He definitely had his work cut out for him.

The "bodies" were mostly mismatched collections of squished flesh in rubber bags. They'd need DNA matching to avoid Frankensteining them—families tended to frown on that, even though these would all be closed casket funerals. With two notable exceptions, Detective Sherman—a bit of makeup would hide the clean entry wound in the middle of her forehead, and a new wig would disguise the messy exit wound—and the neighbor, Zephyr something or other.

When the coffee finished brewing, Grais poured himself a cup and went into the examination suite where the bodies waited. Figured he'd start with the easiest one, give the java time to work.

Grais broke the seals on the body bag. "Examination of Zephyr Rubens," he spoke into the recorder.

And began the long, involved process of the modern forensic autopsy.

Grais was familiar, passingly, with what had occurred—none of the news reports made a ton of sense, seemed like there'd been an earthquake, coupled with a few feral individuals running amok. There'd be time to catch up on all the gory details later.

He had his own gory details to attend to.

Grais photographed the body, cut off her clothes, took scrapings from under the nails. Other than the bruising around her neck, she seemed fine. Rigor mortis had not yet set in, so the job wasn't too difficult.

Finally, the initial stages complete, Grais took a scalpel and began a Y-incision, cutting shoulder-to-shoulder.

"No blood," Grais said. "Curious." He cut around the breasts, curving down towards the pubic bone—

CLINK.

Grais frowned. That was not a sound one usually heard when autopsying a human body.

Perhaps she's ingested something, Grais told himself, although he was nowhere near her stomach.

Still, a consummate, hungover professional, Grais finished making the incision, then used the scalpel to peel back the skin. A dusty, mustard-yellow cloud rose up from the cavity, Grais coughed into his mask, waving a hand to make the haze dissipate.

Nothing about it made sense. Gripping the scalpel, Grais swallowed and peered into the woman's body.

And goggled at the impossible sight. Instead of tendons, organs, and viscera, he was looking at two-by-fours, studs, frayed wires. Grais blinked, trying to square the sight before him with his thirty-odd years of rooting around inside human bodies.

He could not.

Which is why, in the morning, an orderly found him slumped against a wall in the examination suite, gibbering to himself.

Both eyes gouged out by the bloody scalpel, still clutched tightly in his hand.

ACKNOWLEDGEMENTS

Big thanks to:

Max Booth III, for his editing prowess.

Lori Michelle for the incredibly easy-on-the-eyes layout.

Matthew Revert, for the super dope cover and interior sketches.

My agent, Jennie Dunham.

Bottle Logic, Green Cheek, Pure Project, Pariah, and the 4th Horseman, for keeping me fed and buzzed during the writing of this MS.

To Jasper Wilson, for teaching me how to poison a man and get away with it.

You, especially, for reading this book, and if you don't mind maybe give it a review on Amazon and Goodreads?

And Jaclyn, for everything, always.

ABOUT THIS DUDE

Brian Asman is a writer, editor, producer and actor from San Diego, CA. He's the author of *I'm Not Even Supposed to Be Here Today* from Eraserhead Press and *Nunchuck City* and *Jailbroke* from Mutated Media. He's recently published short stories in the anthologies *Breaking Bizarro, Welcome to the Splatter Club* and *Lost Films*, and comics in *Tales of Horrorgasm*. An anthology he co-edited with Danger Slater, *Boinking Bizarro*, was recently released by Death's Head Press. He holds an MFA from UCR-Palm Desert. He's represented by Dunham Literary, Inc. Max Booth III is his hype man. Find him on social media as @thebrianasman or his website www.brianasmanbooks.com.

Here's a picture he drew of a haunted house:

WEEKS LATER

SOMEWHERE, THERE'S A new housing development under construction. Phase One's a couple hundred units, nice big yards looking out on quiet, tree-lined avenues. They just laid the cement for what's going to be the neighborhood pool.

Close to shopping, a good school district. There's a multiplex and a mall just a few miles away, though not so close traffic's spilling over.

Perfect place to raise a family.

Phase One's almost done, but the foreman figures somebody in corporate must've started Phase Two without telling him because one day he's driving by the expansion site and sees a model home.

Doesn't quite match the blueprints he's been working from, but it's nice. Solid construction. He parks in the driveway, sidles up for a better look. The landscaping crew obviously hasn't come through yet, because the yard's just dirt and gravel, a couple odd ruts scored in the earth.

The porch creaks under his weight. The swing rocks. He peeks in the living room window.

Place is already FURNISHED.

The foreman stalks off the porch, dials his boss. Gives the man what-for about hiring someone else to do Phase Two, and is there some kind of problem with his work, because LISTEN PAL—

He's blue in the face by the time he reaches his truck, still screaming epithets at a cowed and confused Director of Operations who's struggling to get a word in edge-wise. He never sees the woman watching him from the hallway window.

After a time she turns away, walking stiffly into the master bathroom—she can still feel the insulation stuffing her wounds, the section of pipe replacing her lacerated intestine, the spackle holding her throat together.

And the broken towel rod, fused into her shattered spine.

A bath's already been drawn for her.

Her body isn't what it was once, nor her life.

But she still loves a good bubble bath all the same. She pulls the cashmere sweater over her head and sinks into the bath.

Alone with her House.